THE STRIPPER

BOOKS BY MICHAEL HEMMINGSON

FOR BORGO PRESS / WILDSIDE PRESS:

The Rose of Heaven
In the Background is a Walled City
How to Have an Affair and Other Instructions
Barry N. Malzberg: Beyond Science Fiction
Auto/Ethnographies: Sex, Death, and Independent Filmmaking
Sexy Strumpets and Troublesome Trollops
The Yacht People
Seven Women
Hold Me, Please, and Say This is Love
Give Me the Gun, She Says
Judas Payne

FOR OTHER PRESSES:

The Naughty Yard (Permeable Press, 1994)
Crack Hotel (Permeable Press, 1995)
Minstrels (Permeable Press, 1997)
The Mammoth Book of Short Erotic Novels (Carroll & Graf, 2000)
The Mammoth Book of Legal Thrillers (Carroll & Graf, 2001)
Wild Turkey (Forge, 2001)
The Comfort of Women (Blue Moon, 2002)
The Dress (Blue Moon, 2002)
My Fling with Betty Page (Eraserhead Press, 2003)
Drama (Blue Moon, 2003)
The Rooms (Blue Moon, 2003)
The Lawyer (Blue Moon, 2003)
House of Dreams Trilogy (Avalon, 2004)
The Garden of Love (Blue Moon, 2004)
Expelled from Eden: A William T. Vollmann Reader (Thunder's Mouth Press, 2004)
Short & Sweet (Blue Moon, 2006)
William T. Vollmann: Freedom, Redemption, and Prostitution (McFarland, 2008)
Star Trek: TV Milestone (Wayne State Univ. Press, 2009)
Gordon Lish and His Influence on 20th Century Literature: The Life and Times of Captain Fiction (Routledge, 2009).
The Reflexive Gaze of Critifiction (Guide Dog Books, 2009)

THE STRIPPER

A Tale of Lust & Crime

by

MICHAEL HEMMINGSON

The Borgo Press

An Imprint of Wildside Press LLC

MMIX

For Sage

1.

Hadn't seen Melody Johnson in almost eight years—since we were fifteen and sophomores in high school; that night, at a party in Ocean Beach, we recognized each other among the stoned, drunk, laughing people and we embraced like old friends, old lovers really. She kissed me on the cheek and I touched her long, straight hair (that smelled like cigarettes) and kissed her on the forehead. She hadn't changed all that much; her once golden blonde mane was now platinum with a purple streak; she still had the swimming pool blue eyes and pointy little nose with scattered freckles that made me fall in love with her when we were kids—when we were both trailer park trouble-making white trash punks in El Cajon.

El Cajon, if you don't know, is the asshole of southern California.

"Well," she said, holding a cigarette in one hand and a beer in the other, "look at you," stepping back and giving me the long and slow once over—something she did with everyone back in our days of wayward youth.

I'd changed; I wasn't as skinny, or tweaked on meth, or pimply. I had muscles and tattoos acquired in prison. I had a tan, from working outdoors.

So when Melody Johnson asked where I'd been all these years, I didn't hesitate to tell her: "Inside."

I knew she'd understand. "County or state?"

"Both."

She nodded and took a drag off her smoke.

"So," I said.

"Me too, in a way," she said, exhaling. "Inside."

"Yeah?"

"Been in L.A. the past three years, doing movies."

"You're a star?"

"Not the normal movies you take the rug rats to…."

I nodded.

"You understand?" she said. "I think you of all people should…."

"Yeah," I said, a little uncomfortable now with the memories, "I certainly I do."

"But, I couldn't even cut it as a porn actress," she laughed, sipping her drink, "so I did the usual thing and ran back home. *Here.*"

San Diego. I came back because I'd never been anywhere else and didn't know where I could ever go….

2.

Melody's uncle—Pete—always said one day she'd make a fine porn star, or stripper, or whore: all three. He'd say it was her destiny, just like his sister: her mother. Oh, he'd say these things—starting when she was nine or ten—as he took nude photos of her and fondled her and kissed her....

3. I'd always been a small-time criminal and didn't have any ambitions to graduate to bigger counts.

Heists, bank robberies, blackmail, moving large amounts of hard drugs—while guys I knew went that route and either were sent away for ten, fifteen, twenty years or got themselves killed (or got themselves rich)—that wasn't my *thang*, man. "The Retirement Score is a myth," said my prison compadre, Ron Hoagland, in Concoran State, "so don't you *ever* buy into that." I didn't. "It's like the lottery," he also said, *"one* lucky sucker in a zillion's gonna get it, but we're not *all* gonna get it, and it ain't worth even trying." Oh, I believed every word Ron said, and took it to heart to keep me out of trouble—that is, until Melody came back into my life....

...and she told me about her plan for a big score.

4. It didn't happen right away, just like that—snap of the fingers and Melody and I were lovers again

(like we were picking up where we left off). It didn't even happen the night we met at the party (seemed we both knew someone who was a friend of someone going to that gathering); there, she gave me her number and said we should catch up on old times, etc. Took me a week and a half to call her—at first I was afraid to; then I didn't

MICHAEL HEMMINGSON

want to; then I forgot about her; then I was looking in my wallet and found the little piece of paper with her number on it so I picked up the phone and dialed.

"I was wondering when you'd call," she said—her voice was cracked and I knew she was on a cell phone. "Thought you hated seeing me or something."

"I was just...things got busy," I said. "Um, you know."

She said, "I guess I wouldn't blame you."

"It not that," I said, "really."

"So do you have it in your little brain to take me out to a movie and dinner?" she asked.

"I—"

"Yes?"

"Well—"

"Because if you *do*, buddy, all I have to *say* is," she coughed, "*I'd love to*. I *really* want to see that new Clint Eastwood flick—"

So that's what we did.

It was like a date. And then we went and got pizza at that little place in Lemon Grove which we loved in high school; the owners were Greek and the pizza was Greek; sitting there, it was like eight years had never happened because the same family ran the place, the food was just as good. Only thing different was the price was higher and we could legally order beer and she didn't have to dread going back to the trailer park and dealing with her coked-out uncle climbing into her bed.

"So, Georgie," she said after two slices of pizza and three bottles of Michelob Dark, "What have you been doing with yourself after getting out of the ol' pen?"

"Staying away from trouble."

"I hope so. You have a parole officer and all that?"

10

"Yeah."

"He a jerk?"

"She's okay."

"She?"

"Yeah."

"I hear they're all hard cases."

"She is. But she's all right as far as they go."

My P.O. referred to herself as "pragmatic" when we first met.

"What do you do for work?" Melody asked.

"Gas station."

"You pump?"

"Fix brakes and change oil."

"I remember," she said with a soft smile, "you liked to work on cars. You'd fix people's cars at Hidden Paradise."

Hidden Paradise was the name of the trailer park we lived and grew up in. El Cajon—paradise—*right.*

I asked her what she did for work and Melody shrugged and said, "This and that, you know."

The "date" was nice and I wasn't sure what to expect; after all, here I was with the girl who once said she loved me so I figured she'd invite me back to her place, or we'd go to mine. I had no idea where she lived and she didn't tell me.

"Hey, I *really* dig this car," she said about the 1972 Mustang, running her hand along the hood.

"It was a project when I got out," I said. "I rebuilt her myself."

"Her. Men always call their cars—"

"Like ships."

"She's a beauty."

"She's getting there."

"Don't let her hear *that*."

I drove Melody from the pizza joint in Lemon Grove to the movie theater at the Grossmont Trolley. She had her car there, a beat-up, old little Datsun Z-40 two-seater.

"Hey, I had fun," she said, kissing me on the cheek.

"Good night," I said, watching her climb into her car.

"Drive safe," she said.

Then she reached out her window to take my hand.

"Call me," she said.

5. On our second date, a week later, I met her at a miniature golf course in Mission Valley. She was wearing a long leather jacket, her pockets filled with small bottles of Skyy Vodka and Wild Turkey. We got decently drunk, which is the only way to play miniature golf. The evening ended in the parking lot with a long, sloppy kiss—a five-minute smackeroo—the kind of smooch seen in the romantic movies, you know; the kind of lip-locking we did as anxious teens in a different life.

"I had fun," she said.

"Me too," I said.

6. She invited me to her apartment for our third date, which was three days later. "I want to make you dinner," Melody said on the phone. I wasn't going to argue with that. "I'm *actually* a good cook," she said, "believe it or not." I believed it and she proved it; she made this sweet and sour chicken with brown rice and

vegetables; we drank a six-pack of Hemp Beer and switched to Bushmill's whiskey. She had a tiny one-bedroom in Pacific Beach, five blocks from the ocean. "Sometimes, late at night, when I wake up and can't go back to la-la land," she said, "I can hear the waves crashing, and it sounds so nice. I move my body and the bed moves and I feel like I'm out on the sea, I'm like a pirate—yo-ho-ho-arragh—and that puts me back to sleep." She had a waterbed. Sex on a waterbed was—interesting. Unless you're used to it, it's not easy—you have to match the rhythm of fucking with the motion of the little ocean.

7.

For the next week and a half, I went over to Melody's twice and she came over to my studio apartment in Golden Hill once; we fucked and slept in each other's arms and it was nice...I hadn't been with a woman—other than a call girl I'd called up the day after I got out of the joint—in more than two years. I'd really only had two girlfriends in my twenty-three years: Melody and then Rhonda when I was nineteen. Rhonda OD'ed and died when we were both twenty. I loved Rhonda but I can't say what I felt for Melody was love because we were just kids, jaded punks really who never thought we'd live out high school let alone graduate. Turned out we just didn't graduate but here we were, and holding Melody in my arms I thought that maybe I could love her, it was possible; if this new thing between us was going somewhere. I was afraid to bring it up and the world I came from, men didn't bring that shit up. Men fucked their women good and hard and got their dicks sucked and never concerned themselves with matters of "a relationship."

8. Melody's tattoos mesmerized me—colorful against her white skin, an eagle with spread wings on the small of her back, a falling angel by her left shoulder and a snake going up her right leg, and a small crucifix below her navel. I would lick and kiss the ink on her flesh; when she was asleep, I would admire the craftsmanship. She said she got them in L.A. "Although tats aren't so popular in porn anymore," she added.

9. I guess it was just a thing. Melody stopped returning my calls and when I did get her on the phone, she was distant, said she was busy, said she'd call me back. It hurt, sure, but I would never let her know how much. I stopped calling and even stopped thinking about her when I jerked-off. Which wasn't easy...

10. The night I decided to erase Melody Johnson from my brain, I went out to get drunk, knowing lots of booze would aid me in my goal. I did not want to drink alone in my tiny place—that would just depress me. I walked down to The Turf Club, a bar and grill hangout where they served your steak, hamburger, chicken or tofu patty raw and you had to cook it yourself on a fire grill in the middle of the joint. I liked their hefty Long Island Iced Teas, where I planned to have many. The place was packed. I started to have a conversation with a tall—five-foot-nine—rockabilly chick named Eve. She had many tattoos up and down her arms, on her chest and breasts, on her back and belly. A few hours later, when she was naked in my futon, I traced my fingers over the tats on her ass and by her shaved pussy. "I'm the illustrated woman," Eve said, "every one of them has a story...."

11.

I liked Eve, and Eve liked me, and that was totally cool. When we both woke up with hellish hangovers and looked at each other and realized what happened during our mutual drunk, there wasn't any embarrassment or hard feelings. I watched her get dress, she wasn't shy about it. I told her how much I liked her tattoos and she said, "Thanks." She said, "We should do this again, okay?"

12.

So we did it again, and again—*and again.* Two weeks into it, I figured I'd found myself a new girl. Until Eve's ex-husband showed up. Now here's a story—

Eve and I were going at it on her waterbed, I was on top, she said, "Holy shit fuck shit," pointing at the window—

A guy with greased-back black hair was staring in, looking at us; he was pissed and mumbling to himself. He started to pace back and forth, cursing loudly.

I jumped up and pulled my pants on.

This guy removed the window screen and leapt into the bedroom like a superhero, like he knew what he was doing, like he'd done this before. He was a rockabilly guy: the greased hair, the black muscle-shirt, the tight jeans, black boots, and many tattoos on the arms.

"What are you doing?" Eve said. *"Just what the fuck do you think you're doing?!"*

"You porking this silly-ass dork?" the guy said, pointing at me, looking me up and down.

"Get out," Eve said, but she said it softly.

"Who *are* you?" the guy asked me.

I said, "Who are you?"

"Adam," he said, "her husband."

"That's *ex*," said Eve.

"We're bonded forever, woman," said Adam.

"Wait a minute," I said, "Adam and Eve? Are you fucking kidding me?"

"Dude," he said, "you're dead."

"Bring it on."

We fought. Eve watched, but she had a smile on her face. I got in a few good punches but Adam kicked my ass. I tasted blood, my face was swollen, I was lying on the floor and holding my balls, which were in extreme pain because Adam had kicked them hard.

Adam spat on me, said, "Dork."

"Baby, baby, baby," Eve cooed, "you get me so *hot*!"

Adam joined her on the bed and they began to have vigorous and rough sex.

I gathered the rest of my clothes and left.

13.
I slept for a day and went back to work and told myself the hell with women, no more women, they're nothing but trouble...

14.
"The job going good?" asked Sandra O'Connell, my parole officer, crossing her legs, her fingers templed.

I tried not looking at her legs, covered in black stockings like smooth paint.

"Yes," I said, "very good."

"How about your personal relationships?" she asked, running her tongue over her lower lip. "Are you dating anyone?"

"No," I said, "no one."

I told myself to not have any fantasies about my P.O.—she was in her forties, she was as old as my long lost mother, and she had the power over my freedom or going back inside.

"But if you do," Sandra said, "you'll tell the young lady the truth?"

"Of course."

"Like we discussed."

"Yeah."

"You're doing good."

"I hope so."

"I like that."

"I'm glad."

"Keep it up."

"I'll try, ma'am."

"Hey."

"What?"

"What did I say?"

"That I have to keep my shit straight."

"No 'ma'am' stuff."

"Right. Sorry."

"I hate the insinuation."

"I'm sorry."

"It's okay."

"I forget, you know."

"It's Sandra."

"Sandra."

"Good."

"Thank you."

"You can go now."

"Thank you."

"Hey," she said.

"Yes, Sandra?"

"I'm proud of you," she said, and winked.

15.

A week later, Melody called. At midnight:

"Georgie."

"Hello?"

"It's me," she said.

"Oh, hey," I said.

"Are you mad at me?"

I didn't reply.

"Do you hate me?" she asked again.

I said, "No."

She said, "I wouldn't blame you."

"I'm not mad at you," I lied.

"Good."

"I don't hate you," I said, happy that she was on the phone.

"That's good," she said.

Silence.

"Will you meet me?" she asked.

"Why?"

"You *are* mad at—"

"No," I said.

"Meet me, okay?" she said. "We need to talk," she said....

16.

She suggested an ice cream parlor downtown. It stayed open late for when the bars closed. Drunk people liked ice cream, and so did we. Melody had a waffle cone and I had a banana split.

"Just like the good old days, huh?" she said. "When we'd go to the Frostee Freeze...."

I nodded and she looked sad. She had dyed her hair a bright burgundy since I'd last seen her. I liked it, and I wanted to tell her so but I started to wonder: what was the point? Men complimented her, flirted with her, tried to seduce her all the time, and she was jaded about it. She was gorgeous and she knew it, she didn't need anyone to affirm this.

"The good ol' days," I said.

She said, "Well, I guess those days weren't so 'good' and not that 'old.'"

"No," I said, "guess not."

"You *are* mad."

"No."

"I can tell."

"Maybe a little," I said.

"It wasn't my intention to hurt you," she said.

I lied to her with a shrug.

"I didn't mean to brush you off or not call you back," Melody said. "It's just—I got into this weird head space. I was down and I mean *really down*. I couldn't see you, not when I was that black in the brain. So I shut the world out, and then I decided to go to Los Angeles and see some people I didn't want to see, that I shouldn't see.... I ran away from that scene once but like a fool I lapsed. But, anyway, I'm back," she smiled, and licked her cone real sexy-like, "I'm here, and I'm alive, and I'm feeling a little better in the noggin."

I asked, "What happened?"

She shrugged.

"You can tell me."

"No," she said, "I can't."

"Okay. That's cool."

"Let's just forget this sour interlude and pick up where we left off. Is *that* cool?"

Something told me to tell her no—to walk away—but I said, "Yeah, sure, I'd like that."

"Do you know what *I'd* like?" she said, touching my leg and squeezing. "Georgie boy?"

17.
We went back to my place and fucked for hours and it was so goddamn good like it's supposed to be good.

It was gratifying for me. For Melody, sex was something else—it always had been thanks to her pervert of an uncle....

Pete—

18.
In the dark, lying on my futon, the air thick with sweat and sex, Melody said, "I feel like I *can* talk to you about this. Only you would know. You're so sweet," she said, touching my face, "my Georgie boy."

"What?" I said. "What is it, girl?"

"Why I freaked out and went dark," she said, "why I ran back to L.A."

"Tell me," I said, "talk to me, girl."

"It's my uncle, my sonofabitch uncle."

"I thought he left San Diego."

"He did. Then he came back, and then he went to jail for six months and when he got out he looked me up and he wanted to crash with me and of course I told him where to go. But he started to stalk me, hang around, and knock on the door, so I moved. I moved to L.A. because I figured he'd never be able to find me there. It's a big place and every corner you turn, there's a girl just like me: running away from something. So I knew if he did try to find me...."

"Did he?"

"No. And when I came back, I heard he was in prison for assault, a bar fight or something. He blinded the man he was fighting, with broken glass. When you told me you were inside, the first thing I thought was: 'Did Georgie boy do time with Uncle Pete?'"

"Where's he—?"

"*Was* doing time. He just got out. He was in Chico."

"I wasn't—"

"I know," and she touched my face again.

"So he's out," I said, "and did he try looking you up?"

"No. Not yet. But I'm sure he will."

"Does he know where you live? Your phone number?"

"No, but he's resourceful."

"How did you hear he was released?"

"Oh, a little bird," she said.

I didn't push it.

"My worst nightmare is that he'll walk into where I work and see me and laugh—you remember that horrible screech of a laugh—"

"Yeah," I said. "Where do you work, anyway?"

"I didn't tell you...."

"No."

"I'm dancing, three nights a week, at The Body Shop."

"All nude."

"Better money. Have you been there?"

"It's been a while."

"Are you surprised? Shocked?"

"Why would I," I said.

"I know you understand," she said.

"I do, girl," and I did.

"And you know my uncle likes strip clubs. *That's* my nightmare. He'd see me shaking my ass and say: 'I always *said* this is what you'd be good at....'"

She snuggled against me; she wanted to be held and I held her.

"I *am* good at it," Melody said, "but the *last* thing I need to hear is that coming from his big ugly mouth...."

19.

Like I said, Melody and I knew each other when we were fifteen. I noticed her before she even knew I existed, even though she was in two of my classes (Biology and English) and lived with her mother in the same trailer park where I lived with my dad and his girlfriend—*friends*, actually, because there was a new one every six months or so, and every one of them was a drunk or an addict...and, to me, ugly. I'm not talking about looks, although to me these were not appealing women. They were vampires sucking off my father; he always needed a lady around to, as he said, "grab a beer, cook up some grub, and suck the dick." Melody, it goes without saying, in my eyes, and the eyes of many boys *I'm sure*, was far beyond ugly—which is why she never noticed me. I was a skinny heavy metal kid with long hair, acne, and a lot of Slayer, Iron Maiden and Led Zeppelin t-shirts. Melody was what you expect from a trailer park chick—super tight pants or short skirts, tank tops and no bra and blonde hair and pink skin, always with a cigarette and booze on the breath and always a lot of lipstick and make-up. She noticed me when I started carrying a bird on my shoulder, a cockatiel named Gypsy. Gypsy was a gift from one of my Dad's girlfriends, Carlee; the only transitory pseudo-mom I really liked and who was around the summer before tenth grade but disappeared just after New Year's. Gypsy was a Christmas gift, eight weeks old, gray with yellow and red circles on her cheeks. Carlee kept saying, kept telling my old man, that what I needed was a pet. "The kid needs something to take care of," she said, "to love, and the creature will love him back..." But my father hated dogs and said a cat would stink the place up with litter and shit. "I want to get him a pet for Christmas," I heard Carlee say one night, while I was lying in bed and glad I didn't have to hear them having sex in the other bedroom. So my dad said something like, "Get him a turtle or a snake," and on Christmas Day, Carlee presented me with the cockatiel.

"Her name is Gypsy," said Carlee.

"You named the bird?" said Dad. "Georgie is supposed to do that—I mean, it's *his* bird, right?"

"*She* told me her name," said Carlee.

"What? The bird?"

"Yeah."

"How?"

"She communicated this to me."

"The *bird* talked to you?"

"In a way."

My dad laughed. "Woman, you're crazy."

"So they say," said Carlee, who made money by working at a psychic phone line and doing private Tarot card readings. "Her name is Gypsy," she told me, "but if you want to call her something else—"

"I like Gypsy," I said.

"Just make sure the damn thing shits in one place," said my father, "and keep a lot of newspaper under it."

20.

It was Gypsy who caused Melody and I to become friends. I brought my bird to the biology class, because we were doing a week of aviary studies. I told the biology teacher, Mr. Klass, who was a cool old guy, about my cockatiel and he said, "Bring her, it'll be like show and tell." Melody Johnson and Gypsy seemed to fall in love with each other—well that's what I thought when Melody came up to me and said, "Oh what a pretty bird, aren't you afraid she'll fly away?"

Gypsy was sitting on my shoulder and jumped on top of Melody's head.

Melody went, "Ohhh!"

"Sorry," I said, reaching for my bird.

"No, it's okay, it's awesome," said Melody, "it's totally rad. This," she laughed, *"is really cool."*

I remember hoping to God that Gypsy would not take a crap on this hot blonde girl's head.

"Hey," Melody Johnson asked, "don't you live by me?"

I said, "Yeah."

She smiled and Gypsy chirped.

And that's how we got to be friends—how we became lovers is another story....

21. Melody liked hanging out with me, and it goes without saying I did not mind her company or attention, but we didn't kiss or fuck and if I tried she would have probably laughed at me. Or so I thought.

22. I wasn't a virgin—I'd lost it at thirteen to one of my father's girlfriend's: her name was Jan and she had muscles. Yeah, she liked to lift the weights. She came into my room one night when Paps was out with Carlee (long before Carlee moved in because Jan was in the trailer) and said: "I'm gonna make you a man, *boy*." And so she did. It was nice and strange. Two weeks later she vanished like all of Dad's women....

23. Tommy was this guy who was sixteen but still a freshman because he kept flunking or getting into trouble. He lived in the trailer across from me with his grandmother, an old woman who drank wine all day and had no idea about the petty thefts Tommy committed and the drugs he used. Tommy always had pot or acid but my thing was crystal meth and he knew plenty of people who cooked and sold the shit.

El Cajon was, and still is, crystal meth central in San Diego; on hot days you could walk down the streets and smell it being cooked, and I used to joke I could get a contact high from the air.

Tommy had long shaggy blonde hair and was a true rocker. He loved Black Sabbath and introduced me to Pink Floyd.

One day, while his grandmother was out playing bingo, Melody and I found ourselves in Tommy's room smoking some weed and drinking cheap beer and listening to *The Wall*. Tommy couldn't keep his eyes off Melody's body—she acted like she didn't know, or care, and I was trying to hide that this made me feel weird. It was difficult *not* to look at Melody's form: she was wearing cut-off jeans, her ass cheeks hanging out; and a blue tank top, no bra. She was drinking twice as much beer, but little pot— and she did two lines of meth with me.

We were fucked up and loose and Melody started to dance to the music.

"You sure look fine," Tommy finally said.

"Thanks," she said, dancing.

"Take your clothes off," he said, "strip for us."

"Ha, ha."

"Really."

"Ha, *ha*."

I was wishing she'd go, "Sure," and do it. I so badly wanted to see her naked.

"I hear you *fuck*," Tommy said, "is that true?"

I couldn't believe he asked her that. I expected Melody to stop dancing and get pissed off, but she just smiled and said, "Yeah? Where did you hear that, Tommy boy?"

"Around."

"Around where?"

"You know where."

"You don't know dick," she said.

"Oh come on," he laughed.

27

"What do you think I am?" she asked.

"I dunno, babe, what are you?"

"Don't call me that."

"Babe."

"That's not my name."

"Slut."

She stopped smiling, but continued dancing. "Well, you're wrong. I don't fuck, not casually. Fucking is for love."

"Yeah," Tommy said, "you ever been in love?"

"The question," she said, "is: have *you* ever?"

"Yeah," Tommy said, "I'm in love with you right now and I wanna fuck you. Georgie's is love with you too, can't you tell?"

She stopped dancing and smiled, deviously. "Tell you what," she said slowly, "I'll give you both head. Will that make you horny boys happy?"

Tommy was quick to unzip his pants and pull out his cock. "Here it is," he said, "suck it dry, slut."

I still couldn't believe this was happening. She went to him, got on her knees, and did it. Tommy came quickly. Melody turned to me and said, "You're next, Georgie." I was frozen but excited and my prick was hard. Melody crawled on her hands and knees to me and that just made me crazy with lust because I could see down her tank top, I could see her white tits and pink nipples. "It's okay," she whispered, "don't be shy, it's cool, I like this," and she pulled my pants down, took my dick in her hand, looked at it for a moment, and then put it in her mouth.

Tommy watched, opening a beer and smoking a bong hit.

Being young virile men, Tommy and I were immediately ready for more. He wanted to fuck her but she still said no.

"You still don't believe I love you?" Tommy said jokingly.

"I *don't* love you," she said seriously, "I'm not even sure I *like* you."

He laughed.

She said, "But I'll suck you guys until your balls are totally dry."

"Oh you're *wicked*," Tommy laughed.

24.

Later that day, Melody said to me, "You must think I'm terrible now."

"No," I said.

"I can tell."

I didn't know what to say.

She said, "Sometimes when I get stoned...."

"It's cool," I said.

"It's *not* cool," she said. "I wish it was just you and me, not you and me and him."

I wanted to hold her, I knew she would like this but I was too inexperienced and young to know how to do this...right.

"I don't really want to party with Tommy again. I know he's your friend and all, but he reminds me too much of my uncle."

"Okay," I said.

"We can still be friends after...?"

"Yeah," I said.

"Cool," she said, brushing her hand against mine.

25.

"She's a *slut*, a *whore*," Tommy said, "everyone knows that...."

"She's awesome," I said. I didn't want to talk about Melody with him.

"She's probably done half the men here in Hidden Paradise," Tommy said, laughing, cutting up lines of meth on a mirror, using one of his grandmother's cancelled credit cards.

"Yeah?" I said.

"Yeah," he said.

I didn't believe him.

"I don't think she likes me," he said.

I didn't reply.

"She likes *you*."

I tried to not let that show.

"But be careful, dude," Tommy said, "with chicks like that."

"Like what?"

"Oh come on," he said. "I've talked to her uncle. I bet he's done her. The way he talks about her. He says she's a whore like her mother is a whore. Hey, would you do her mother?"

"Me?" I said. "No."

"I would," he said, and laughed, and snorted up a line.

26. I'd seen Melody's uncle come and go—one day he was there, living with them, and then he'd be gone for a while; then he'd come back, and then he'd be gone....

27. ...and one sunny day, Tommy was on some poisoned acid and *really bad* speed and feeling mean, at least that's what I heard. He came across a neighbor's cat that'd just delivered a litter of five kittens. He used a knife to slit the mother cat open and behead all the kittens. The woman who owned the cat caught him and tried to stop him but Tommy stabbed her twice—he didn't kill her but he hurt her bad, and the cops were called. I didn't see this happen—I heard Tommy was laughing the whole time and didn't resist arrest.

I never saw him again.

"Good riddance to bad rubbish," Melody said when she heard the news.

28. Melody disappeared for a week and a half. She wasn't in school, her mother didn't know where she was and didn't seem to care.

"Sometimes she does that," her mother told me, smoking a cigarette and drinking from a bottle of Southern Comfort, "she just ups and goes. She says she gets dark in the head. She's probably just off some with guy. Or are you her guy? Are you her beau? You don't seem the type, she likes the boys with muscles and bikes. But you're always around. Speak up, young one, are you her man or what?"

"I'm worried about her," I said.

"Don't be. You wanna blowjob? Get your dick hosed? See these teeth? They come out. If you've never had a gum job, *you've never had a blowjob*," she laughed, drinking.

I laughed too, just so she wouldn't feel insulted. "Next time," I said.

"Any time," she said.

29.

Melody did finally return—back to Hidden Paradise and school.

"Where were you?" I asked.

"Nowhere," she said, and from the look she gave me I knew not to press it.

30.

Later, she would tell me that she was off getting high with her uncle and some friends of his—who paid money for the good time....

31.

"I missed Gypsy," Melody said, "can I see her?"

Melody and my bird had some weird kind of a rapport—Gypsy had even learned her name. In a high-pitch tone, Gypsy would say, "Mellludiiee!" This always delighted the girl I now had such a great crush on, it hurt in my chest.

Melody would stick out her lips and Gypsy would put her beak to those lips for a kiss. Cockatiels like to kiss. Gypsy would kiss me all the time but in my head I was always thinking of Melody kissing me...she'd given me oral sex but I'd never kissed her. I'm sure if I wanted kisses she would have given them to me, but I was afraid. And what was I scared of? Rejection, I guess—what every teenager fears—

32.

One horrible day, I was walking around with Gypsy on my shoulder and she jumped off. I don't know why she did this, she never did this, but the wind and the fact that I hadn't recently clipped her wings made her fly. I was walking down an alley and she jumped into a backyard...and there was a dog. I leapt over the fence but the dog had Gypsy in its mouth. I yelled at the dog. A big, fat guy, not wearing a shirt, with lots of tattoos on his arms and chest, came out with a shotgun. A small blonde woman with a baby in her arms was behind him. The baby was crying. The guy pointed the shotgun at me and said, "Don't move."

"Your fucking dog is killing my bird, man," I said, trying to fight off the tears.

The baby was crying....

The small blonde woman said, "Hank, he's right, there's a bird...."

"Aw shit," Hank said, *"Buddy, drop that now!"*

The dog growled and let go of Gypsy.

Gypsy fell to the grass and was making horrible sounds.

The dog, Buddy, wanted my bird back in his slobbering K-9 mouth.

"HEY!" Hank yelled. "BUDDY, NO!"

Hank lowered his shotgun and looked genuinely sad.

Not as sad as I felt.

"Aw shit, man," Hank said.

I picked Gypsy up, I held her in my hands. She had two puncture holes in her back, and blood was coming out of those holes.

"Shit, man," said Hank, "there's a vet half a mile away, I can drive you there, maybe they can do something...."

I knew there was nothing a vet could do.

Gypsy bit my thumb, hard; so hard she drew blood—her last act. Then she died.

33. I walked home, carrying my dead bird. I kept hoping, wishing, she would come back to life, that something divine would happen.

34. The weird thing was, Hank and I had history. When I was twelve, one hot August, I was walking down the same alley and saw a small woman with long blonde hair lying topless on a blanket in the same backyard that Gypsy died; there was no dog at the time. This woman had wonderfully perky tits with long hard nipples and you can imagine what that was like for a twelve-year-old boy. I stopped and stared—just stared and I could not help myself and my dick was hard. Still, I stood there and ogled this pretty woman; she turned her head and saw me and she yelled, "HANK! HANK!" and Hank, big and fat but without his shotgun, came out, saw me, and said, "You better run fast, boy, or I'll kick your little ass!" and I ran. I ran home and jerked-off, thinking of the woman's tits.

35.

—and so, another weird story, I met Hank again: after I got out of prison and before Melody came back into my life. I was at a bar on University Avenue, in North Park, having a few when I noticed a large, beer-bellied man sitting alone at the counter, on a bar stool. Oh, I recognized him all right; he had not aged well the past decade. I don't know what made me sit next to him—probably because I was drunk and I didn't give a shit. I wondered if he'd identify me from his past but, of course (like I knew) he did not—I was not the twelve-year-old who'd spied his woman's knockers or the fifteen-year-old whose cockatiel had died from the jaws of his dog.

He looked at me and said, "Hey."

I said, "Hey."

He offered to buy me a drink, and then I bought him a drink; we bought each other a few drinks and shot the crap.

He eventually told me that his first wife, a brunette, had left him for another woman. "I had no idea she was a fricken dyke," he said. Then he told me that his second wife wouldn't let him see his son, and the courts couldn't help him. "So what's *your* story?" he asked.

"Just got out of the pen," I said, "and trying to get my life back on track, you know?"

"Yup—been there."

"How long?"

"Five years. You?"

"Two."

"Two too long," he said.

"Yeah," I said.

"Man, I don't really miss my ex-wives, to be honest," he said. "I *really* miss my dog, Buddy. Dog's man's best friend, y'know."

I said, "Yeah," and smiled into my drink—

36.

—but the thing was, what my secret was, I had killed his dog. It was, after all, revenge....

37.

Anyway—Melody saw me walking back to Hidden Paradise, holding my dead bird, blood on my hands and tears in my eyes.

She came up to me, wearing a little white dress, showing a lot of leg, and said, "Hey, handsome."

I was afraid to let her see my face.

"What is it?" she asked.

I couldn't speak.

She looked at Gypsy and said, "Oh my God."

She cried too.

We both cried, and she helped me dig a hole in the dirt, there in the trailer park—Gypsy's grave.

38. My father was off with some new girlfriend and I knew he wouldn't be back until morning, or the next day. Melody stayed the night with me; she laid with me on my bed and held me and kissed me and we cried together like parents who'd lost a child.

"Georgie," she said, "I want you to know that I love you, I mean I think I love you and I think you love me, too."

What could I say to that?

"Yeah?" she said.

"Yeah," I said.

"So I wanna make love with you," she said, and we did.

39. "I hate dogs," Melody said, "they're evil."

"I always wanted one," I said, "but now I never...."

"You have to get even," she said. "Revenge is the only way. Revenge will make you feel better."

"I want to," I said.

She kissed me and said, "So do it."

"How?"

So she told me how—

40.

Melody helped me stuff a lot of small shards of glass into a piece of thick eye of round steak that we got at the local Albertson's Grocery. We drank some beer and Southern Comfort—her mother's stash—and at two in the morning, wearing dark clothes, walked down to the alley in question and stopped at the backyard where Buddy, the bird-killing dog, lived. Buddy barked. I tossed the steak over the fence. Buddy yelped and quickly gobbled the meat up. Melody and I sat down in the dirt and waited; it took about half an hour before Buddy started to whimper, fall down, and cry out in pain. Lights were turned on in the house, I heard Hank say, "Buddy, what's your problem?" Melody and I, holding hands, ran away; we ran back to Hidden Paradise and her mother was gone so we went into her room and made love.

"Do you feel better?" she asked.

"Not really," I said.

"But you avenged Gypsy," she said.

"Yeah."

"So you *should* feel better."

I did, but I didn't want to admit it.

But in the morning, I felt just awful about the dog. What did he know, right from wrong? He was simply doing what nature told him: grab the bird.

Took me three weeks to brave walking down that alley again; when I did, there was no sign of Buddy. I went down the alley for a month, almost every day, and never saw the dog again....

41.

"You have to get even," Melody had said. "Revenge is the only way. Revenge will make you feel better."

So later, when we were adults, when we were together again, she asked me if I would help her take care of her evil molesting uncle, all I could say was: "Yes."

"Yes?"

"Sure, baby."

42.

Baby. What is it with these terms of affection?

43.

"My uncle never called me anything nice or sweet," Melody said, "it was always 'slut' or 'cunt' or 'whore.'"

44.

Back to when we were kids—Melody's mother was arrested for solicitation and possession of heroin while hanging out on Magnolia Avenue in El Cajon, where many whores worked at the time. Because of priors, her mother was going to do a year and social services wanted to put Melody in a foster home. Her uncle showed up, he was clean-cut and convincing and told the court he was capable and willing to be her legal guardian. Melody's mother signed off on this, Melody didn't say anything otherwise, and the judge agreed to the arrangement. So her uncle moved into the trailer and paid the rent and no one in authority knew Melody's uncle had been raping her since she was—

"I'm not sure when it started," she told me, "but I was either nine or just turned ten. Does it matter? *He has to pay*."

45.
"I hate that sonuvafuckenbitch," Melody told me while we were under the covers in my bed, "I hate what he's done to me and what he's put in my head."

She told me this: when the sex started, when she didn't know better and her mother wasn't around, her uncle convinced her that what they were doing was love; that it was okay; that uncles and nieces all over the world did this and it was natural—she believed this, and she felt she loved him. Despite the pain, she did what he wanted because he brainwashed her to accept it. He would disappear for weeks, months, the come back, sleeping on the couch but coming into her room. It wasn't until she was thirteen that she realized he was also going into her mother's room too....

"Something wasn't right," Melody said.

"So why do you let him go on?"

She cried into my chest and said, "I don't know how to tell him…."

She said, "It's all I know…."

She said, "And he makes me screw men for money and I hate it, I fucking hate it…."

46.
Twice, Melody asked me to kill her uncle. Once, when we were fifteen—

"Help me murder him," she said, "like we did to that dog—"

"That's crazy," I said.

"No," I said.

"We'll go to prison," I said.

Next, when we were twenty-three—

"Help me get revenge," she said.

"Why?" I said. "Do you know what kind of trouble we can get into?"

"Because he's not just my uncle," she said, "he's also my father. *The bastard fucked his own sister and got her pregnant and that's why my goddamn mother never told me who my daddy was!*"

47.
When we were almost sixteen, Melody's mother was killed in jail during a fight with a Chicana gang—shanks were used. When the news came, Melody's uncle told her the truth: that he was her father.

In the night, she packed her things and left. She didn't even leave me a note.

When I was seventeen, I was arrested for stealing a car and did two months in juvie. I was back inside six weeks later for breaking into an arcade to steal coins from the games.

So began my life of little crimes....

48.

Melody's uncle had somehow gotten her cell phone number. "Honey," Pete said, "let's get together and talk."

She was scared, afraid he'd find out where she worked, where she lived.

"Talk, smalk," she said, "he just wants to try and *fuck* me again, like I'm some stupid little girl."

"Call the cops," I said.

She gave me a disgusted look.

"I don't trust the cops, what can they do?" she said. "I have to kill him," she decided. "Will you help me this time? *Will you, lover?*"

"How?" I asked—weak, so weak....

49.

"This is what I'm thinking, Georgie," she said. "You work with cars, you know how to fix them...."

"Yeah," I said suspiciously.

"And you also know how to *un*-fix them, then, right? You know how to—look, this is what's going through my head: a car accident, a mechanical failure. His car will crash, and the asshole will die, die, die."

"Listen," I said, "I'm on parole. Something like that— not only is it a parole violation, it's murder. I'd get twenty-five to life. I might get Death Row."

"Oh that's crazy," she said, hugging me and kissing me on the forehead, "because you *won't* get caught. You won't leave fingerprints. The cops will never know—he had bad brakes is all."

"They'll know."

"He's a crook, he just got out himself—he has enemies. You think the cops are going to care two shits about a piece of fuck like him?"

"If I even got caught doing anything to his brakes, that would send me back inside. Is that what you want? You want me to go back to prison?"

"I want you to *love me*," she said, knowing all the right words, "and I want you to help me."

50. The weakness of men when it comes to women—much has been said and written over the centuries on this subject. There are plenty of songs, movies and paintings, too. *And* there are plenty of guys in the joint.

Sex—what people will do for it, what prices they have to pay. Because I did not want to lose Melody's affections and because her pedophile uncle violated her when she was just a child, an attempted murder was about to be committed on the streets of San Diego.

I called Melody on her cell at one A.M., when I knew she was getting off her shift at The Body Shop.

"Okay," I said, "I'll do it."

"Thank you," she said, softly.

"Listen," I said.

"You listen—I'm coming right over and I'm gonna give you a night you'll never forget...."

51. A note about Melody's dancing job—she didn't want me to go to the club and watch what she had to do for a buck. "I don't want you to get jealous if you see me give some fat smelly ass-hole a convincing smile, like I like him," she said. I told her not to worry, I didn't like to go to those places and I *didn't* want to see her working in one, either.

52. Uncle Pete lived in a real shit hole—a falling apart one-bedroom in Normal Heights off 34th Street and El Cajon Boulevard. The paint was chipped all over the house, the grass and weeds were uncut and I doubt hardly any sun shone through because there was a massive tree in front of the property, leaning toward the one-bedroom shit hole. There were numerous feral cats wandering around the night I went there at 3:30 A.M.; I could smell their crap and piss in the grass and weeds and they all scattered about and mewed as I made my approach. There was a twenty-year-old Ford truck with souped-up wheels and hydraulics, dark blue with faded flames painted on the side, parked on the dirt driveway; I remembered this truck well and it was easy—too easy—to slip under the vehicle, shoo away a couple of curious kittens, and cut the brake line with a small knife. He'd have enough fluid to back out and drive a few blocks and not notice something was wrong. The idea here was that he'd get on the freeway, or before the freeway, and when he pressed on the brake pedal, nothing would happen. I hoped—said a little prayer even—that no one else got hurt. No one innocent. Uncle Pete—*Daddy*—was not innocent.

53.

I called in sick to work—I'd never done this before and while my boss wasn't too happy, what could he do? "Get yourself well, man," he said, "and I'll see ya tomorrow." I hadn't slept a minute; I was worried as all fuck. I was waiting for the cops to come to my door. I'd used gloves, I was certain no one had seen me but the cats...but *still*. Still. *Shit*, what was I thinking? I laid in bed all day, too afraid to turn on the TV or the radio. Felt like the eyes of the whole city were looming over the apartment building, waiting for me to step outside and point fingers at me and yell: "There he is! He did it! Toss him back in the pen!"

A little after four in the afternoon, my phone rang but I didn't pick it up.

Melody's voice, excited: "Hey, you there? Where *are* you? Georgie? *Yo, Georgie.* Hey, hey, hey. Pick up. If you're there—"

Grabbed the phone. "I'm here."

"I saw it on the news, did you?!"

"No, what?"

"The accident this morning—"

"Are you sure—?"

"Just a quick mention but I knew it had to be him and I was sneaky, I asked around—"

"Asked? Asked who?"

"We shouldn't talk on the phone," she said. "I'm coming over."

"Wait," I said but she hung up.

She was at my door in twenty minutes.

I checked into the peephole to make sure it was she.

She was wearing a purple mini-skirt, knee-high boots, and a tank top.

"It's stuffy in here," she said, "open a window."

She opened a window.

All I could do was look at her ass.

"So," she said, and told me that Pete's truck lost control as he got off the freeway, heading to work.

I sat on the futon. "Did anyone else get hurt?"

"No; thankfully, huh?" She sat next to me, a bare leg wrapped over mine. "He went down an embankment; his truck rolled a couple of times and he was thrown out."

"Is he dead?"

"No. He's in the hospital. I don't know his condition, but I can check on that. I'm *family*, aren't I?"

"Do you think that's...?"

She smiled.

I shook my head.

"Thank you for doing this, boy," she said, playing with my hair.

"But he's not dead."

"If he's crippled or in a coma, that's good enough revenge for me. Hey," she asked, "why are you so sweaty?"

"I called in sick."

"You're not sick."

"I'm supposed to be."

"You need a shower, boy; go take a shower," she said; it was a command more than a suggestion. She leaned in close to my ear: "Then we'll go to my place and I'll make you a real nice big dinner and then—*then*," she kissed my cheek, "we'll *get low-down and kinky*, okay?"

54.

Melody made a pizza—she got the pre-made dough from the grocery store and slapped on hefty amounts of mozzarella and cheddar cheese, pepperonis, sausage, Lingüiça, garlic, bell peppers, olives and pineapples. She added hot dogs too which I thought was funny but she said, "You just wait and see, this tastes great." She was right. It was the thickest pizza I'd ever had and I had to use a fork so it all wouldn't fall apart, dripping cheese and everything. We had some beers and then vodka and started to make out. I told her I was so bloated I wasn't sure if I'd be able to fuck, I might have a heart attack with all the cholesterol running through my blood. She patted my bulging gut, said, "I have *just* the thing to get you hot, because it always gets *me* hot."

She went to the bedroom. I kicked back with a smile, expecting her to return naked or wearing something made of leather; she came back with half a dozen porn videos in her hand.

"I never showed these to you, what I did for work in Los Angeles," she said.

"No," I said, "you didn't."

She sat next to me, sporting an insidious grin, showing me the boxed videocassettes. I was confused, but definitely interested.

She said, "I wasn't sure what you'd think, that's why I never showed you my little porn movies."

"But you told me...."

"It's not like how I don't want you to come see me dance. This is totally different...."

"How?"

"I've done many, but these are my top favorite...."

"How is this different?"

"Dancing disgusts me because I have to look into the eyes of the creeps who watch me and I know what's going on in their puny sponge matter that they call brains. The porno, I get off watching them; I *love* to watch them all the time...."

Melody made it clear that she was obsessed with this: watching herself get fucked.

"Do you want to see?" she asked.

I did, yes, but there was something in me that did not.

"Sure," I said, "lights, camera, action, girl."

"Some I have just a scene, others I'm the star. Which do you want to ogle first?"

"Anything," I told her, "whatever."

The first two tapes were just scenes; in one she did two men in a classroom setting and another she had a lesbian scene with an older woman—she was the babysitter, and the older woman's husband observed as he jacked off.

Melody was aroused as she watched, and watched me watching—she touched me, kissed me, and touched herself....

The third video was centered on Mandy O'Canyon, her porn star name (or one of them); it was called *Into Mandy's Many Doors*. Mandy was a young lass who, through the accident of sex-crazed aliens, started moving through the doors of alternate universes—her life (or sex life) different in each...and, of course, in this journey all her "doors" were penetrated by many cocks. In one universe, she only got off by giving blowjobs; in another, she only liked it up her ass. The flick ended with Mandy doing a gangbang with all the men she met, as well as the aliens.

As we watched this eighty-minute movie, Melody slowly undressed, masturbated, undressed me, and stroked my dick with her moist hand.

"I *love* watching myself fuck," she said and I have to admit: so did I.

55. There were twenty-two videos in all (or so she said, I'd learn otherwise later on), and eventually we watched all. For some, she gave me extra copies so I could view them when I was alone at home.

Did I?

Yeah.

56.
I went back to work like I never tried to murder a man. Melody and I continued seeing each other like we did before.

I wish it could have stayed that way, but shit like this never does....

57.
"So...how are things?" asked my parole officer, crossing her legs and leaning forward.

"Things are the same," I said with a shrug and a grin.

"Good?"

"Good, yes."

"Good," she said, writing something in my file...

58.
"Tell me about prison," Melody said. "About being...*inside*."

"What's there to tell?"

"A *lot*."

"Not really."

"I mean it must be hell."

"It is at first," I said. "But you adapt. You take it day by day."

"Like A.A.?"

"I don't know. I guess."

We were lying naked on her bed. She wrapped a shapely white leg over my crotch, played with my hair, kissed my ear and said, "You can tell me. Did you have to...?"

"Was I punk?" I said, amused.

"Is that what they call it?"

I laughed uncomfortably; this was something I *didn't* want to talk to her about.

She said, "It's okay."

"I wasn't...but that doesn't mean some assholes tried."

"Does that thing happen a lot?"

"Depends."

"On what?"

"Lots of things."

She leaned back and looked at the ceiling, a wandering and sexy hand between her legs. "I used to have this intense fantasy that I was thrown into a jail cell with a bunch of big mean dirty smelly burly men; I was forced to do all kinds of nasty filthy gross things; I was ravished and violated and molested in so many ways...."

"Sounds like a porno movie," I said.

"One day I wanna do *that* video," she said, and giggled, and kissed me all over my face.

This is when I knew her adult entertainment days were not quite over....

59.

Anyway. Prison. *Not* the days I like to dwell on.

I'd done my short stints in juvie as well as a month or two in jail, after I turned eighteen, for bullshit like petty theft, trespassing and possession. It was only a matter of time that I graduated to something big which would result in some real time. My Dad said, "It's inevitable, the way you're going...." I didn't know what that word meant, *inevitable*, but it sure did happened. I turned twenty-one and I didn't have any money to celebrate so I robbed a liquor store with a fake gun; got away with $412 and spent it all on speed and beer. Got myself on the security camera too, and it was only a matter of days when the cops came to get me. I was in a foul mood and took a swing at the cop trying to put the cuffs on me; I got him good, his lip was bleeding, and then he proceeded to beat the shit out of me and his partners just stood and watched. I was told I had it coming; I asked my public defender about charging police brutality and she said, "Forget it, it won't go anywhere. They have you on tape, and they're offering a deal: plead guilty for the armed robbery and they'll drop the assault."

"I wasn't even really armed," I said. "It was a toy—"

"Doesn't matter."

"What will I get?"

"Three years, it'll be state prison, but you'll only do half if you keep your nose clean."

"What if I want to go to trial?"

"You could do seven to ten, another year for hitting the cop."

"I didn't—"

"Look," the P.D. said, "take the deal, okay?"

I sighed and said, "Okay."

My Dad only visited me once, before I went to court to get my sentence.

"I have to turn my back away now," he said. "For good. Even when you get out."

"I know," I said.

"You understand?"

"Yeah."

"You don't, but you will some day."

"I fucked up, Dad."

"Yeah, you did."

"So now I gotta pay."

"When you get out, maybe you'll learn something, maybe you'll know never to fuck up again."

As I was being processed at the prison, a guard came up to me and said, "You knocked out a tooth of a buddy o' mine."

"He was a pussy," I said, and smiled. "Like all you pigs."

The guard slugged me in the gut.

I went down.

He kicked me in the face and I lost a few teeth.

"Welcome to Concoran, ass-pussy," the guard said.

Concoran. Charles Manson was there, but I never saw him. I heard the actor Robert Downey, Jr. did a year there; I heard he sucked a lot of dick, but I didn't believe it.

The Aryans and Mexicans looked at me and made it known that I would soon be sucking dick and taking it up the ass. I started pondering on how I would make myself like it, just to survive. I'd never been punk'd in juvie, I always fought my way out of that and I never had the desire to make some kid my bitch. But a friend told me, "If it happens, you gotta get out of your body, take your mind somewhere else, especially if they gang you."

So my first day in the yard the Aryans came after me, eight of them, big with shaved heads and shit-eating grins. Okay, I told my brain, get ready to go somewhere else. But a tall guy in his forties, with long hair and arms covered in various tattoos of dragons, women and devils, stepped up and shook his head. He didn't have to say a word; the Nazis stopped, stared at him, then me, and then him.

"Want him for yourself, Ron?" one said, and then they all laughed.

"He's off limits."

"Your bitch then."

They turned and left.

The guy looked me up and down.

I asked, "Should I blow you right now?"

He smiled. "You ain't my type, kiddo."

"So what do I owe you?"

"Walk with me."

We walked.

"I'm Ron, Ron Hoagland."

"George...."

"I know. Your old man, we go way back."

"You do?"

"I knew your mother, too; she was a friend."

"Is that so," I said, wondering what kind of friend.

"You don't remember me, I used to come around," he said. "Last time I saw you, you were eight-years-old and playing with Tonka trucks."

"So who are you?"

"A friend. I owe your old man. He said you were coming here, and I said I'd make sure you didn't get killed or get your asshole turned inside out."

"Thanks," I said.

"Hey, it's the least I can do, kiddo," he said, and slapped me on the rear....

60.

"Ron was in for strong arm bank robbery; a small bank in a desert town called Hemet, $12,000 take," I told Melody, because she wanted the details. "He took off to Sacramento and the state cops caught him a month later. He had priors and was sentenced to ten years, and was on his sixth when I got in."

"So you didn't remember him when you were a kid?" she asked.

"No, but I don't remember much from birth to about the age of eleven. Ron—he saved me from experiencing a lot of grief and for that I was grateful; he was a part of my past so we had a, um, connection. Some of the inmates figured I was his bitch. I didn't care what the fuck they thought."

"But you weren't?"

"No."

"I wouldn't think any less if—"

"I didn't take *any*one's dick," I said.

"So was Ron some kind of top guy in there? Did he have connections?"

"None that I knew of. He wasn't with a gang, no one ever visited him, and no ever messed with him. But he was a tough bastard, tougher than anyone I've ever met."

"Muscles?"

"Plenty, but lean. Oh, some new guy would try to fuck with him, and Ron would take the stupid asshole down in less than ten seconds. I was amazed at his moves—some weird combo of martial arts and street fighting. And he'd hurt them bad—broken legs or arms, one guy was crippled for life. And no one would rat on Ron. The guards knew, but they figured the other guy had it coming. One time he did get caught in a scuffle so he was sent into the hole for thirty days."

"The hole?"

"Solitary. They stick you in a rubber room with no lights, naked and with only bread and water for food. I never went but I knew it was no day at the park. So he was gone for a month and it was the worst month there. I was expecting to get it from some gang or dude at any hour, and I was given these looks, but nobody made a move."

"Because you were Ron's 'bitch,'" Melody said, taking delight in saying this, "and they knew when Ron got out...."

"Yeah well," I said, feeling funny, "so what. As long as they kept away from me...."

"Ron had respect in there."

"Sure. He was also the heroin liaison, so maybe that had something to do with it. Mess with him, the heroin supply was cut off."

"Oh? Tell me more."

"Why?"

"It's fascinating."

"No, it was pathetic."

"You never did heroin?"

"Not in there and not in the world. You?"

"Tried it a few times. Not my thing."

"Not that I'm any kind of saint," I said. "I did drugs in prison—crystal, coke, moonshine...."

"Drugs are easy to get in there?"

"Easier than out in the real world. The guards are paid to look the other way and I'm sure the warden was getting a kick back, he couldn't be that stupid. Who knows. But Ron was the guy who put it all together. He always said he was just a middleman, a negotiator, he never got his hands dirty. He knew the people who could supply the best stuff, and other guys greased the guards and had people on the outside that could get the shit inside. Ron got some kind of cut, no one messed with him, he had his position of power and he watched everyone destroy themselves on smack. He didn't do the shit, told me not to do it, and would say: 'Let these sons-of-bitches kill themselves, the world is better without them.'"

Melody nodded and said, "This Ron sounds very smart and very cool."

"He is."

"I wouldn't mind meeting him some day."

"You just might," I told her, "he's up for parole soon."

61.

I'd never talked to anyone about my prison days, or about Ron—not even to my parole officer, like she'd care. It was nice to talk to Melody about all this—to have an ear and to get it off my chest.

There are two things I left out, though—

One: that Ron arranged the death of the Mexican gang leader who was causing trouble. I don't know how, but Ron had the Mexican's smack tampered with and the guy's heart stopped when he shot up.

Two: the day before I got out, I asked Ron, "Tell me the truth, was there something between you and my mom?"

Ron nodded, said, "It was short, it was nothing, it was before she met your dad and you were born. But we remained friends, and your dad and I got to be pals."

"Thanks for telling me."

"Your mother," he said, "was a beautiful woman."

"I don't remember," I said, and: "Wish I did."

"Take my word on that, kiddo."

62.

Melody's uncle didn't die in the hospital. In fact, he got better pretty fast and although bandaged up and unable to go to work, he was sent home and a nurse came by once a day to bring groceries, check up on him, give him a sponge bath and, Melody said, "probably blow him like he used to make *me* blow him every day I got home from school."

"How can he afford a nurse?" I said. "Did he have a good insurance policy?"

"That doesn't matter," Melody said, frantic, "what *matters* is that he's *alive* and he *shouldn't* be alive. Do you *understand*, Georgie?"

"Yeah."

"Do you?"

I was irritated. "Yeah," I said, "I do."

"I *don't* think you—"

"I understand what *I* have to do," I said, and she smiled and kissed me on the nose.

"Okay," she said.

"Okay," I said.

63.

I didn't plan it out. I didn't hesitate. I did the job that night. At 4 A.M., when I was certain that Uncle Pete would be sound asleep, I went to his place and killed him. I put on a pair of gloves and walked up to the door, prepared to use a credit card (like you see on TV) or smash it in with my foot (like you see in the movies), but the goddamn door was unlocked and ajar. I heard a TV, a Tony Roberts infomercial that reminded me of my crystal meth days when I'd stay up all night and stare mindlessly at infomercials. Pete was on the couch; he was on his back and snoring, the TV light flickering over his body. Spit dribbled out of his mouth and he farted. A bottle of Jim Beam, almost empty, sat on the floor. He looked desolate, miserable, stupid—and I hated him: I hated him for what he'd done to Melody; I hated him that he came back to San Diego when he got out; I hated him because he didn't die when his truck crashed and I hated him because I had to be here and do this. This revulsion helped me to take a pillow out from under his head, place it over his face, and smother the motherfucker. *Just like in the movies.* He put up a small fight but I sat on his body and pressed the pillow down hard until he stopped...he stopped fighting and he stopped breathing. I didn't take the pillow away to look at his face. I didn't want to see his face. I was confident that he was dead. I had given Melody the ultimate gift any man can give a woman: erasing the sins of the past.

Right now I had to deal with the sins of the present. It was Melody's idea to make it look like a robbery. So I started to thrash the place, careful to be quiet so the neighbors wouldn't hear any sounds. I turned up Tony

Robbins' excited, motivating voice on the TV and knocked down a lamp, turned over the kitchen table.... I went into the bedroom and opened the dresser drawers.... I found a small bag of cocaine, $200-300 worth.... I pulled clothes out of the closet. On the closet floor, there was a brown paper bag. I opened it and there was money inside. Lots of money, in bundled tens, twenties, and hundreds.

Holy shit.

64.

"Holy *shit*," said Melody Johnson when I showed her the cash.

We counted it. $15,540. Exactly.

Melody held up some of the bills, especially the larger ones, examining them in the light, wrinkling them up in her palm and smoothing them out.

"It's real," she said, "not funny money."

"How would you know?"

"Oh I just know."

"Yeah," I was amused, "how?"

"I've seen counterfeit money before," she told me, "and I can tell the difference."

"Tell me more."

"I'll tell you later."

I shrugged.

She giggled.

"Now we know how he can afford a nurse," I said, "but where did he get this cash? Why would he work if he had this dough?"

"It's not really *a lot*," she said.

True.

"Hey," I said.

More than I'd ever seen at one time....

"It's nothing to turn your nose up to," she agreed.

"Maybe he was saving it," I said, "maybe he couldn't get a bank account because he was a con. I had the same problem—"

"Doesn't matter," Melody said with a cold look on her face.

I said, "No."

"He's dead, *right*?"

"Right."

"You're sure, boy?"

"I'm *very* sure, girl."

"We're killers now," she said.

"Right," I said.

And I was scared.

This, I knew, was a good thing.

65.

I was scared and I was paranoid. I was expecting the cops to come and get me—I'd used the gloves but still...*still*. There was nothing on the TV news but Melody found it in the *Union-Tribune*: a small story about an apparent break-in and murder. Maybe drug related, it said.

"So he *is* dead," she said.

"I told you," I said.

"I'm gonna fuck you *so good* tonight, boy," she said, but sex wasn't on my mind....

66.

A sentence for twenty-five to life *was*. And the needle. Melody said she understood, like I knew she would. We *did* understand each other, after all. She said, just to be on the safe side, we should lay low—I should quit my job and move.

I agreed wholeheartedly.

"And maybe we shouldn't see each other for a while," she said, "in case the cops come around and ask questions. I'm his niece, or that's what they think, so...."

"Right, right," I said, "good idea."

"Later, things will be okay."

"When."

"Soon, boy, soon...."

67.

We split the fifteen grand, but not equally—Melody took five and left me ten. She said I needed it more than she did and she was right. She didn't want the cocaine and I figured it might come in handy some time. I quit my job and asked my boss not to tell my parole officer. Being an ex-con himself I hoped he'd understand and he said, "Okay, I won't. You're good with cars, so you'll be missed. I just hope you're not in trouble."

"Nah," I lied, "I just—"

"No need to explain. Good luck to you."

I was sorry I had to split from that job too; my boss had been good to me and I liked working there but if any shit started to fly, I didn't want it to go down at work.

I packed up what little I owned—clothes, a little TV, a boom box and a lots of CDs—and I moved into a cheap motel downtown San Diego, which was just a mile or so from Golden Hill.

I knew downtown pretty well, although it'd changed some since I went to prison—more "upscale" and there was the new ball park and a lot of condos being built, but there were still the motels, hotels, and SROs for the down-and-out, the lost, the lonely, and those who needed to hide.

I hated them all, these sorry-ass excuses for homes—which is why I moved about from one to the other those months after freedom....

Let me tell you about some of them—

68.

The Workman Hotel, on 14th and J, offered rooms about the size of a jail cell. I lived on pizza slices, shredded beef tacos, and the candy-dispensing machine in the bleach-scented hallway. Many of the residents on the five floors were prostitutes, crack-heads, just-new-in-town or, like me, recently released from the pen—or the bughouse. Like the six-foot-three woman who lived in the room across from me said, one night after I shared my pizza with her (softly like it was a national secret): "Keep your eye out for the robots." *What robots?* "Those damn robots who zap into my walls every night and tear my arms off! I know what you're thinking: 'But her arms are still on!' Let *me* tell *you*, those *robots*, after they *cut* my arms off, *they sew them back on!* So watch out and keep safe, okay?"

The Baltic Inn, on Fifth and Island, provided cable—the best thing about the place, really; having many channels to choose from is a good thing during those lonely SRO nights. The rooms were stuffy with small windows and the front desk staff acted like they were manning the station of a three-star joint and never failed to try to put "the make" on any single female residents (there were a number of foreign students staying there, a lot of women from France, Germany and Japan) all of whom usually ignored the standard pick-up lines. There must have been an avid reader of popular fiction in some room, because every Tuesday and Thursday I would find, in the front lobby, a pile of broken-spine paperbacks: science-fiction, mystery, historicals, and thrillers. Seemed like I was the only one who picked up these mass-market tomes, and this is where I first read the works of Greg Bear, Andrew Vachss, and Bill Pronzini. One of the front desk clerks asked if I liked the abandoned books; I replied that most weren't bad. "Me, I never read fiction," he said; "I prefer biographies and works about history. I prefer reality," he said.

The Coast, on Seventh and Island, was a notorious crack hotel, so much that the local news often covered the court battles the city waged against the owners to shut down the crappy building. Periodically, the cops would place a mobile trailer station half a block away; I never saw any arrests made, the police wanted the crack dealers to know *they* were there and *watching*. The dealers were not intimidated—in fact, they were amused. "Yo, 5-0!" they'd yell at the police with wave of the hand and a cackle from the throat. I would up living and working there after walking by the puke colored building, half-dazed from hunger,

and seeing a sign that said **HELP NEEDED –
TRABAJO**. I walked in and said I wanted to apply for the
job. "Can you start tonight?" they asked and I said yes, yes
I could. It was the night watch, a twelve-hour shift from
seven P.M. to seven A.M. The pay: a free room plus $100 a
week. At least I could now tell my parole officer I was, for
the most part, employed. It wasn't much, but better than
any other offer I had on the table at the time. I lasted on
that job for three and a half weeks; took me a week to fig-
ure out there were ways to make a few extra bucks, like
getting kickbacks from the dealers who used the hotel as a
distribution center, as well as the prostitutes who brought
their johns in for half an hour of fun. The white whores
lived on the first floor, the transsexuals on the second, and
the blacks on the third. In the very back of floor one, in
what I guessed used to be a broom closet, lived a tall, thin
man with a thick beard who was obviously nuts; his SSI
check paid his rent and he had absolutely nothing in his
abode, except for a few old candy wrappers and faded T-
shirts. Every once in a while his apparent wife would visit
him—she was just as loony; one evening while there was
lightening and thunder in sky, causing them to both laugh
uncontrollably and dance in circles, chanting that God was
sending them secret messages. Two cops showed up another night, asked me about a certain blonde prostitute
called Lana. "Is Lana around? Do you know who Lana is?
She's a whore," the cops said. I told him I hadn't seen her
around in several days, her rent was due, was she in trouble? "Nah," one cop replied, "she just gives the best head I
ever had."

Another time a short balding guy with a big mustache
wanted to enter the hotel, he said he was a cop, he said a

65

whore had taken his "buy" money. He quickly flashed some kind of badge but I knew he wasn't 5-0; I knew he was a gullible john looking for rock or weed who'd been burned of his cash. I wouldn't allow him inside, I didn't want to deal with the trouble he was ready to cause. "There are a dozen men, a SWAT team, ready to bust in the back if you don't let me pass," he said, pissed-off.

"What's your code name?" I asked.

"What's that, asshole?"

"Your code name," I said. "I have to check you out first."

"Cobra," he said. "If you don't let me in there in two minutes, you'll be charged with obstruction of justice."

I called the police station on 14th and Broadway and asked if they had an undercover named Cobra.

The voice on the other end laughed and said, "Excuse me?"

I explained there was a man here passing himself off as one of San Diego's finest.

"Well," the voice said, "is that so?"

In less than a minute, three squad cars showed up. The guy with the badge in his hand was still there. He tried to run. They grabbed him. Turned out his badge was for Wells Fargo security.

The Golden West Hotel, on Fourth and G, had no TV, no phone, just a bed and a sink and the constant smell of cheap paint. One morning, while walking down the hall to the shower, a Mexican maid whistled at me. I was too tired to feel flattered but smiled at her anyway. Coming out of the shower and going back to my room, she smacked me on my ass. Was this sexual harassment yet? Two nights later, at 3 A.M., my door opened and someone climbed into bed with me. It was the maid, she'd used her passkey. I said something like, "What the—?" and she hushed me with a hand covering my mouth; we didn't say a word to each other for the next hour.

The Maryland Hotel, on Seventh and F, used to be a monument of an older, gentler time—indeed, a landmark. Now it was being renovated for yuppies, lawyers, doctors and artistic wannabes. I liked the room I had because it was big and there was a table near the window I could sit down with some beer and watch the antics and activity down below. There was a wee hour incident, after the bars were closed, that I watched two men fight over a woman in a mini-skirt—she was huddled by a cement trash bin and groaning in fear. One of the men smashed the other guy's head into the sidewalk many times. There was blood everywhere. The cops and paramedics came. If the guy with the bashed head wasn't dead, he had to have serious brain damage or gone into a coma. There was nothing about it on the TV news or in the papers.

Another day, I was walking up Seventh Avenue and saw, from the corner of my eye, a young man jump from the top floor of the Maryland and land to the pavement with an unrealistic thud. Someone called the cops and the body was quickly ushered away. "The Maryland gets at least two-three jumpers a year," I heard an officer say. For three years, the stain of the jumper's brains remained on the sidewalk.

The Callan Hotel, on Fourth and Island, sat on top of the Blarney Stone Pub, whose owners also operated the hotel.

I would pay my rent down at the bar, usually getting a snake bite at the same time (residents got a 10% discount on pints from the tap). The rooms were small but they had cable, if you furnished your own TV. There was a security camera at the front entrance but I wondered whom they were trying to fool, the disconnected cord was an obvious giveaway that the camera was not operational. There was a guy in his forties who lived a few doors down; I don't know if he was ex-military but he always wore camouflage and drove an army jeep that was parked on Island, in front of the hotel. Late at night, when I'd return from whatever I was doing, I would find him scrubbing the carpet in front of his door, rather frantically, with a sponge and soap. He seemed irritated that he had to stop, move, and let me pass. I would hear him for an hour or two, scrubbing away in the hall, and think: what the hell? This went on for weeks so finally I asked him what he was doing, the carpet was *clean*—in fact, the color was faded in front of his door. "You dirty fuckers track all over it!" he said in a low voice with angry eyes, backing me up against the wall. "I won't have your grime near my door! You hear me? I'll fight away your stinking dirt no matter how long it takes!" In the morning I poured coffee grounds on the area in question, crushed them into the carpet with my shoe. Several hours later I heard him scream; it was the most god-awful sound I'd ever listened to.

The Pacifica Hotel, on Fourth between Market and Island, was owned and operated by a Hindu family and sat on top of a club/bar called Café Sevilla, catering mostly to European tourists needed the feel of home. I had a room in the front and I could look down and see the people lining up to go inside the club; they'd glance up at me and wave and I'd wave back and sometimes the women flashed me their breasts as foreign chicks like to do. Many of the transient residents of The Pacifica were European or Latin American, all of them out to party and have a good time in the Gaslamp Quarter. One night I was walking up the stairs and ran into three young women from Germany; they were sharing a single room, they were drunk and laughing and invited me in. I had fantasies of some international encounter of sexual perversity—a porn flick scenario that would have delighted Melody—but the three fraus only wanted to smoke hash, drink wine, and ask me questions about San Diego—where they could go in the day and what they could do at night. I did my best to answer them.

69. *Now*, I was a criminal again and hiding/living in the Las Flores Hotel, on Fourth between G Street and Market. The woman who ran the place was mean, unfriendly, and picked fights with residents just to show everyone who *she* was, and who *they* were. To her, everyone was "a piece of shit that I can toss back onto the street." I believed I was just that, without Melody at my side to remind me otherwise. My third day there, I saved this manager from a resident who was trying to choke her to death; she'd scratched his face up pretty bad and he had murder in his eyes. He was stronger than me and I could tell he was high. I pulled him off her. He turned around to swing a punch but I was quick and ducked—or parried.

"You better get out of here before the cops come," I said, and he did.

The window of my room looked down onto Fourth. Watching the people was always entertaining, noting the way downtown people interacted on a daily basis.

One of favorite hangouts for San Diego's teenage runaways is Horton Plaza, especially the east side on Fourth Avenue between Broadway and G Street, right at my window. They kicked back against the walls, solo or in comfortable groups, insulting or panhandling money from people who walked by; smoking cigarettes or playing cheap acoustic guitars that later wound up in the pawn shops across the street.

One of them, who dubbed herself Tessandra, seventeen and five-foot-one, baggy jeans and white tank top and some tattoos on her skinny arms, spent several hours a day singing solitary with a loud, harrowing voice—a wonder of vocal chords from a small person.

She would choose a spot along Fourth and begin with either a well-known pop-songs or lyrics of her own, and people gave her money.

Small crowds always stopped and listened.

"Why do you do this?" someone from the crowd asked. "All that change can't amount to much for all that effort."

"At least I don't sell my body, like some do," Tessandra said with an attitude. There was a lot of angry energy about her, the way she stood with hands on her hips. "And I don't just *beg* for money," she claimed, "I give something in return."

I asked her to sing a song.

"What do you want to hear?"

"Something original," I said. "Something that belongs to you."

She smiled and looked away and, for a moment, appeared bashful. She closed her eyes, chin up, and began to sing in a deep, charred-by-life tone, lyrics of the ecstasy and necessity of slashing one's flesh with razor blades; typical teenage angst but there was nothing hackneyed about her delivery. People stopped to listen; some were her fellow street kids who cheered her on. "Yeah, girl," they said, "sing that heart out!"

I imagined her accompanied by a guitar, or a whole band. I found myself wishing I were a producer with a label.

I gave her a $5 bill when she finished.

"Thanks," she said, quickly pocketing the bill.

"Got any more cash to hand out?" one of the kids asked me.

I waved him away.

"I'll sell you my youth," the kid said, seriously.

"Leave him alone," Tessandra said, and when the kid sauntered off with a scowl, she said to me: "Sorry."

I asked her what bands or singers she liked—not wanting to say something mundane like: "Who are your influences?"

"I'm into PJ Harvey," she said, "Pink, Gwen Stefani, and Nancy Sinatra, of course."

Of course. "One day you should cut a record."

"Sure," she said, "but every dirty old man who approaches me about that is more interested in getting into my pants. You know?"

She continued to sing. A guy in his twenties with bushy brown hair walked by and said: "Shut up already! You suck!"

Tessandra stopped and glared at him. *What did you say?"*

"I said you suck, bitch!"

"Who you calling bitch? Who you says sucks?! You suck!! You're the bitch!!!"

She was screaming, following him, raising her fists, cursing him; he walking away but she kept after him, past the entrance of the Golden West Hotel. A patrol car stopped and two officers got out. They wanted to know what the commotion was all about.

"He threatened me!" Tessandra said. "He tried to molest me!"

"She's lying," the guy with the bushy brown hair said. "I just told her she can't sing for crap is all."

The cops ran the guy's ID through the system and found that he had a bench warrant for failing to appear for something. They handcuffed him and lead him to the car.

Needless to say, this fellow was flabbergasted and kept uttering: "This is bullshit, this is total bullshit."

Tessandra had a smirk on her face.

"You, missy," one cop said to her, "go on home."

The police cruiser drove away and Tessandra jumped up and down and she said to her fellow street kids: "Did you see that?! I *got* that asshole! That'll teach him for dissin' me!"

They all chortled with her, gleefully.

"Now that's just cold," someone behind me said.

"Hey, you do what you gotta do," someone else said.

70.

I called Melody from a pay phone. "I miss you," I said.

"Me too," she said.

"When will we be able to see each other again?" I asked.

"Soon," she said. "We still need to lay low."

"Any word about anything?"

"No."

"The cops?"

"Nothing. You?"

"Nothing," I said, wanting to tell her about the horrible loneliness.

"You haven't spent all your money yet have you?"

I laughed. "It's only been a week."

"Well," she said.

"What about you?"

"Not a dime," she said. "But I will. I deserve to. I should buy myself something nice. Like a long black leather jacket. What do you think?"

"You'd look great in it," I said.

"We'll be together soon," she said, "you believe that?"

"Yeah."

"Good."

71.

Oh, I could've lived half-decent for the rest of the year on that $10,000. The rent at the Las Flores was $120 a week or $450 if I paid monthly. There were plenty of places to get cheap food and beer. I could see myself watching TV all day, drunk and getting fat.

I could also see myself committing suicide....

72.
I knew I had to find a job. I didn't *need* the job, but I couldn't keep lying to Sandra O'Connell. Eventually she'd find out and if she did, I'd be in violation and have to go back in and do the balance of my time. It wasn't hard to find a job—I landed one at a garage that specialized in transmissions and rebuilt engines. There's one certain thing: in a country where people loved their cars, cars would always break down and need repairs. I wondered what would happen to all the mechanics when the oil in the Middle East finally ran out. I'd be an old man by then—or dead. So...I didn't worry about it.

73.
"Did anything bad happen?" my parole officer asked, crossing her legs in a very sexy manner and leaning forward.

"What?" I said, nervous.

"At your job. Why did you *really* quit? You can tell me. In fact," she raised a brow for effect, "you *have* to tell me."

"I get paid better at this new gig," I said. "I liked the tire and brake place fine, but it's just a matter of economics, you know."

She nodded. "You want to move up, that's good," and she wrote something in my file. "This is a positive step. You want to better yourself."

"Yes," I said, "that's it exactly."

"Well," she said, closing my file, "that's what it's all about: becoming a productive member of society, *et cetera, et cetera*."

"Yes," I said, "that's it, exactly."

74.

Melody said she could give me a few minutes, during her break at work. She said it was dangerous but she felt for me, she said she was yearning for my company and to come by the strip club at fifteen to midnight. "Don't come inside," she told me, "just park your wheels, okay?"

I parked and waited outside the club she was dancing at right now, this one near the Miramar Air Base. She was five minutes late. She got into my car wearing an extremely short leather skirt, fishnets, high heels, a tube top and a whole lot of make-up and perfume.

"Whoa," I said.

"You like?"

"You look like…."

"What?"

"A street hooker."

"Like *all* good hookers, I suck cock in parked cars," Melody said, and she did. She buried her face into my crotch and I leaned back, grabbed her head, and enjoyed every moment. It wouldn't have mattered if she did this or not—I just wanted to be near her.

She sat up and popped a piece of gum into her mouth.

"That was a huge load, boy," she said.

"It's been weeks...."

"Hush."

"I'm not sure how much longer I can take this," I told her.

"We'll get through it. Once it's safe...."

"When will we know it's safe?"

"We'll just know."

"Is there anyone else?" I asked.

"What?"

"Are you...?"

She gave me a look. "You should know better."

"Because it's okay."

"Are you fucking someone downtown?" she said. "Because that's *not* okay."

"There's only you," I said.

"And there's only *you*," she said. "We're in love, right?"

I couldn't speak.

"Right, Georgie?"

"I killed a man for you," I almost yelled. "What do you think?"

"I wanna hear you say it."

"I love you, Melody."

"I know," she said, getting out of the car. Leaning into the window, she said, "Just be patient, okay? Can you be that for me, boy?"

"I can," I said.

She threw me a kiss and walked back into the strip club, her ass swaying to and fro in that tight little leather mini.

75.

"Hey, man, I *know* you," said the girl sitting against a wall on Fifth Avenue, tears in her eyes. "Don't I?" she asked. "I *do* know you," she said, with a bit of a smile, "you're the cool guy who gave me five bucks last week. No one ever gives me that much. All I get are quarters and shit."

Tessandra, the street singer.

I said, "Hey."

She said, "Hey," and stood up, stretched, cracked her back, gave me a sheepish look. "Got another five on you? Wanna hear a song? I'm hungry and it's been a crappy day, dude."

"Why? What happened?"

"It's my birthday," she said seriously. "I'm eighteen and I'm old and I've accomplished nothing in my life."

"Why don't I buy you lunch. How about some lunch? We'll have a big lunch, all you can eat."

She gave me a look.

"To celebrate your birthday," I said.

"Well," she said.

"Hey, it's okay."

"Not always," she said.

"I'm a good guy," I said, "with good intentions."

She laughed.

"What?"

"You're corny, dude."

"Yeah," I said, "I am."

"I like your tats," she nodded at my arms.

"Thanks."

"You seem okay," she said, "I like the sound of your voice. You sing?"

"No."

"You should."

"Don't have it in me."

"Never know unless you try."

"I'll keep that mind."

"So if you wanna buy me lunch," she said, "I'm not about to stop you."

We walked over to the Moon Cafe, where I often had breakfast. It was cheap and better than most of the cheap Chinese places all over downtown. She had a cheese-burger, fries, and some pancakes. I had a grilled cheese and coleslaw.

"So what's your story?" she asked with a smile and a mouthful of food.

I shrugged.

"Everyone has a story, dude."

"But most of them are very dull."

"I can see it in your eyes: you wanna know mine."

"Only if you want to tell it, dude," I said, and smiled.

"I was born and raised in Arizona," she said flatly, "my childhood sucked, my life sucked, my parents were shit-heads, so me and some friends split. We came out here."

"Why San Diego?"

"Why not? It's warm and sunny and not too crowded and it's close to the ocean." She leaned forward. "I'm con-vinced that the closer people are to water, the less weird they are. Inland, they're all creepy, dude."

"You sing...."

She sat back. "No shit, Sherlock."

"Why not L.A.? That's where the music is."

"Music people are here too."

"But the record companies...."

"Fuck the record companies."

I took a bite of my grilled cheese.

"I'm no sell-out," Tessandra said. "My music is for my soul, not for some corporate sales machine."

I nodded.

"In L.A.," she said, "if you're broke, the only way to get by is to be a prostitute or do porno videos."

"Yeah," I said, "that's what I hear."

"So fuck them," and she held up her glass of milk.

"The hell with all the bastards," and I held up my soda in a toast, "and the commercial record companies too."

"But," she added, "being famous and making huge bucks off my songs doesn't sound half bad."

"Not at all."

"Some day."

"I believe it."

"I do too. I have time. I'm young, right?"

No, she was not—not inside.

"These friends you came out with," I said.

"Them," she said and rolled her eyes. "They're long gone. I have new friends now."

"I've seen you with them."

"The runaway kids come and go like gutter trash. I was flopping with some people but that's all shit now. Once again, I'm not sure where I'm sleeping tonight, or all week."

76.

After lunch, we walked down the block to the same ice cream parlor Melody and I had gone to and ordered cones. There was so much about Tessandra that reminded me of Melody—both imaginary and real.

"You can crash with me if you want," I said.

"Yeah?" She gave me the eye. "Do I have to fuck you for this?"

"No, that's not it."

"Oh?"

"That's not what I want."

"All men want pussy," she said softly, "especially young pussy."

"I just wanted to help," I told her. "I thought you needed—"

"I don't need help, dude."

I nodded.

"But I don't turn help away."

"Do you need some money?"

"Yeah, but I don't want you to give me any. I *sing* for my bread. I *work*, you know."

"So sing."

"I'm too tired to...."

We sat there, licking our cones.

"Tessandra," I said.

She said, "Where do you live?"

"Over there," I said, and pointed to the Las Flores Hotel.

77.

I had to slip a $10 bill to the guy behind the desk to let Tessandra up to my room.

She looked around and said, "Well, kinda small but not to shabby. You get cable on that TV?"

"Sure."

"HBO? Cinemax?"

"Nah."

She turned on the TV. "I love watching things," she said. "Like *Law and Order*. Or *Star Trek* and shit."

We stood there and looked at each other.

"Are you going to make me fuck you now?" she asked.

"No, that's not on my mind."

"Liar. Men think about it every ten seconds."

"Maybe so," I said. "But I don't want to hurt you."

She laughed.

"What?" I said.

She said, "I'm beyond hurt."

She said, "You don't know what hurt is until you've been in my shoes, dude."

She said, "God, my shoes hurt...."

She sat on the bed, took off her tennis, and rubbed her feet.

I could smell her feet and they smelled like my days in the El Cajon trailer park.

"You can have the bed," I told her.

"And *where* will you sleep?" she asked sarcastically.

"The floor."

"Hah!"

"Yeah."

"You keep your bed, I'll take the floor. I'm used to the floor. I've been sleeping on floors for...a while."

"So sleep on the bed," I said.

She lay back on the bed. "It's nice and comfy."

"It is."

She asked, "Are you going to rape me, Georgie?"

"I would never do that," I said.

"I believe you, Georgie," she said, and she closed her eyes and went to sleep.

78.

I left the room, feeling odd. I can't say that I was in mind to be a total gentleman. Yes, I wanted to fuck the girl; but I knew she'd been dealing with too many people using her like that—and knowing this hurt me and made me feel like a bad man for having impure thoughts.

I also wanted to save Tessandra from the awful future she was heading toward—but what made me so high and mighty? I was a thief and a murderer.

I was a bad person.

79.

I walked around the block a few times. I stopped at a dark, sleazy joint called the Star Bar, just around the corner from the Las Flores, and had a few beers. An Asian woman in a silver dress sat next to me and asked: "You want fun time, Mister?" I smiled and told her no and left the bar. I went to the grocery store and bought a twelve-pack of Red Hook, some crackers, cheese, hot dogs, and chips. Then I went back to the room.

Tessandra was sitting up on the bed, watching the news on TV.

"Hey," she said.

"Hey."

"There you are."

"Here I am."

"Where were you?"

"Out and about."

"It was strange waking up," she said. "For about twenty seconds, I didn't know where I was or who I was. Then it all came back. What do you have in the bag?"

"Supplies," I said, and started putting them in the small fridge that came with the room.

"Oh, beer," she said.

"You want one?"

"Sure you wanna give me one?"

"If you want one," I said.

"Of course I do."

We drank beer and ate chips and watched TV and kept a comfortable distance away from each other.

80.

"Hey," Tessandra asked, "got any drugs?"

"Drugs," I said.

"Yeah, sure," she said, "oh come on, dude," she said, "I know you're no prude or shit."

"Funny you should ask," I say.

"Because?"

"It so happens...."

"Uh-huh?"

I got out the cocaine Melody gave me, the coke I didn't want to touch—or wanted to save for another time.

"Well, well," said Tessandra.

"You like this stuff?"

"I like anything that helps the pain go away...."

81.

We did some lines and laughed and kissed a little bit and then she got this funny look on her face and moved away from me. She said, "Sorry." I told her it was okay.

82.

"I'll sleep on the floor," she said.

"I can't let you do that," I said.

"It's okay," she said, "bed's just make me...I dunno. I can't sleep well on beds."

"Tess," I said.

"The floor is cool," she said. "The floor is my world."

83.

In the dark:

"Georgie?"

"Yeah, Tess?"

"Is there something wrong with me?"

"Not at all."

"Don't you want me?"

"Go to sleep."

"I can't."

"Sssh."

"You sssh."

We both laughed.

"Can I join you, Georgie?"

"If you want."

"I want."

"Okay."

"Look at me."

"What?"

"Look. I'm naked. Are you naked?"

"No. I could be."

"Get naked."

"Okay."

"This is nice, our naked bodies next to each other."

"It is."

"Know what else would be nice?"

"What?"

"If you kiss me."

"Okay."

"Know what else?"

"What?"

"If you stick that hard dick inside me."

"Yeah."

"Would you like that?"

"I would."

"Tell me."

"Yes."

"Call me 'baby' and 'honey.'"

"Baby...."

"Georgie...."

84. I have to admit I felt like a teenager again and it was like being with Melody back then—the jaded innocence, the hopelessness, the drug-haze frenzy, the knowledge that once morning came, the story would be different....

85. In a post-cocaine-booze-sex-dream, Pete—*Uncle Pete*—came to me. He was wearing a white robe. "What did I ever do to you, Georgie?" he said in this dream: "what the heck did I do to you that made you want to suffocate me with my own gosh-darn pillow, eh?" Then he turned into a big giant rabbit with red eyes and fangs and he chased me through a field of sunflowers....

86. In the morning, Tessandra was gone—her body, her clothes, the rest of the coke and the beer and the food as well as some of my money.

It was 10:30. I felt like shit. I noticed that the duffle bag with Uncle Pete's money was open. The bag was in the closet. I went to it. Half the money was gone—$5,000.

There was also a note, on a small piece of paper in neat cursive:

> *Don't think bad of me. I know this is fucked up. I could have taken it all. This money will save me. I am going to Los Angeles. When I become a famous rock star, I will pay you back 100 times. I love you for this, and for our night together. I will love you forever for saving my life, my darling Georgie.*
>
> *XXXXOOOO,*
>
> *Tessandra Blaine*

87. "Melody," I said on the phone.

"Hey," she said.

"Darling," I said weakly, "baby...."

"What is it?"

"I need you."

"I know."

"I can't take it anymore."

"*Soon*, Georgie," she said, sounding like Tessandra, "soon we'll be together."

I asked, "Forever?"

She replied, "What else is there?"

88. "So," said Sandra O'Connell.

"Same ol' same ol'," I told her.

"And this is good?" she asked.

"What else is there?" I said.

89.
Uncle Pete visited me in a dream, again. "Sooooooo," he went, "you gonna answer me *or what?*"

We were in a small boat, out at sea.

The ocean was calm but I knew a storm was coming our way, and there were whales swimming by fast, afraid of the weather.

"Fuck off and die," I told Pete, rowing the boat.

"I am dead," he said.

"So fuck off anyway."

"Wish I could."

"Go away."

"Where?"

"What do you want?"

"Why did you kill me, boy?"

"Because the world is a better place without you," I said.

And he laughed.

90.
"Know this," Melody said on her cell phone, "I *do* love you, and that's all that matters, that's what's going to get us through this bad period...."

91.

I took $1,000 of Pete's money, checked into a $400-a-night suite at the Marina Marriott, and called an escort service.

"Anything in particular you want?" the woman on the phone line asked.

"A blonde," I said, "eighteen-to-twenty-five, thin but built, sassy but classy."

"We can do that."

The escort showed up fifty minutes later.

She was short, wore a black leather jacket and a purple skirt. Boots, bare legs. She was very blonde.

"I'm Nancy," she said.

"Jorge," I said.

"Heya, Jorge," she said, and walked into the suite, looked around, looked at me, looked at my tats, said, "So what's the story, Jory-noory?"

"What will this cost me?"

"What do you want?"

"Can we kiss?"

"No."

"Will you suck my cock?"

"Sure, but you have to wear a rubber."

"I have $600 to give you," I said.

"You can get more than a blow-job with that," she said.

"I want it to hurt."

"Do you want me to hurt you, or—?"

"Or," I said.

"For $600," Nancy said, "you can hurt me just a lit-tle...."

92. "How old are you?" I asked.

"How old do you want me to be?" Nancy said, batting her eyelashes like a femme fatale out of a bad movie.

"Cut the crap," I said, "tell me the truth, bitch."

"I just turned twenty," she said, cold.

93. Nancy's sweet perfume—which she must've put on all over her wonderful whore's body—lingered on my wretched criminal's body, and in the stolen room long after the call girl departed....

94. Pete came to me in a third dream that night— he looked younger than he was. "What did I ever do to you, man? I'm gonna haunt you and haunt you, I'm gonna keep bugging you until you give me an answer that I'm satisfied with."

"You know what you did," I said, "what you did to Melody."

"Little cunt, little bitch," he laughed. "What did I do to her?"

"You know."

"Tell me her lies."

"You raped her!"

"Is that what she made you believe?" and Pete's laughter became as loud as thunder; he started to expand—he puffed up into a giant snowman that loomed over me and glared down with deep black eyes. "She's a whore like the one you just porked with my money. Hey, are you enjoying spending my money? For a hit man, you work cheap."

95.

"There isssss a man on F Street," sang the portly guy in baggy jeans outside a bar , late in the night, playing a banjo and doing an interesting rendition of "House of the Rising Sun." He looked awfully familiar, especially those tattoos on his neck; I knew that voice as he continued: "And he speaks for Gaaaaawd's son...."

What was his name? Ted? Tad? Theo? Tank?

"Hey," I said.

He stopped playing. "Hey." He recognized me. "*Hey, long time no see*," and he held out a friendly hand, with big toothy smile—well, what was left of his teeth.

Oh yes—I knew him from prison. Same cellblock. He'd said he played the congas when he was on the outside, and that he was also a coke dealer....

"Took up the banjo, I see," I said.

"Took up more than this axe, my brother," he said, "I've taken up the Lord. Things are different now. *Now*, I only sing for Jesus."

"So it seems."

"Do you *know* Jesus, brother, have you *heard* the music?"

"I'm afraid I don't," I said, "and the only music I've been hearing is in there," pointing at the bar.

"Jesus knows *you*," he said, "and he doesn't want you to go into that place of sin and booze, that den of wine, women and devil music! He wants you to hear what I have to say!"

"Good seeing you again, man," I said, and went back into the bar.

96.

"Check out my CD, that's my CD, that's *my* music," said the tall young black guy with a smooth shaved head, walking up and down the aisle of the eastbound trolley, holding a carton of CDs, showing them to unsuspecting riders. "You want it, $7 and it's yours," he said as the trolley stopped at the 62nd and Encanto station.

What the fuck am I doing on the trolley? How did I get here. I was drunk, very drunk, and knowing I couldn't drive I'd jumped on the first trolley that came into the downtown station, thinking it would lead me to Melody Johnson and eventual salvation. It was all a haze, I didn't know what I was thinking. All I knew was that I had to sober up.

"$7 and it's yours."

I glanced at the CD, titled *Chronic Ten-Four*—had the tall young guy's image on it, dressed in running gear and gold chains.

"Rap?" I asked

"Of course it's *rap*, it's *bad ass* rap," he said. "You want it? $7 and it's yours."

"$7? I'm not going to pay that for music I haven't even heard."

"It's good, it's *real* good, you'll like it."

"Well, yeah, you gotta say that because they're your tunes."

"Tunes? I got a producer who does the *music*," he said, "but the words are all mine."

"There's no label," I said, examining the cheap manufacturing. "Let me guess—a drum machine, a keyboard, ProTools, a CD burner and a laser printer for this cover."

He glared at me, eyes large and bloodshot. He grabbed the CD from my hand, rolled his shoulders, and stood up. "You just wait and see," he said, pointing at my face, "in a year or two, I'm gonna be as big as Ludacris or even *Snoop* and you're gonna *wish* you bought my homespun CD cuz it's gonna be worth *a lot*."

He added, "Smart-ass motherfucker," walking away.

I closed my eyes and tried not to think of the pounding headache that was beginning to brew in my skull....

97. Somehow, I found myself in Ocean Beach. I'd found her here before, maybe I would find her again. I needed another drink....

98. "You got a light?" a guy with baggy jeans and a spider-web tattoo crawling up his arm asked, standing outside a club called Dream Street. I hear live music coming out.

"Sorry," I said, "don't smoke."

He nodded and said: "Should quit myself. Grandfather died of lung cancer so that should tell me something."

"Yeah."

"Funny thing," he said, "when I first moved here, someone told me there was a stripper joint. In OBecian Land? They said yeah. Dream Street. But they never went. 'What kind of strippers work in OB?' So I walk over here—I mean I live right down thataway—thinking I'm gonna catch some T&A but it's *this place*. All these bands and it's usually pretty empty but—so what? I like the bands sometimes."

"A stripper club?"

He laughed. "Sounds like one, huh? Dream Street, Dream Girls? Looks like one. *Smells* like one—you know, that bleach smell?"

"Maybe it was," I said, "once."

H shrugged; I shrugged.

"Hey," he said, nodding toward two blonde young women in the parking lot, standing close to one another other and talking with quick and hushed voices, "they look like strippers, huh? Maybe they smoke...."

He sauntered their way....

One produced a lighter and he was smoking.

"It's fucking cold," the one without the lighter said.

"Yeah," the guy with the webs on his arm said, "so what are you babes up to?"

"Our friend's band is playing later, next I think. The one right now really sucks."

The music seeping out into the parking lot was a well-timed 4/4-drum beat, muddy bass and loud, reverberated guitar. Vocals? I couldn't tell. Didn't sound that bad.

"It's gonna be a *cold* night tonight," said the guy, smoking his cigarette and looking east.

I went west, to the beach.

Where I fell asleep.

In the sand.

Woke up at sunrise with sand in my mouth and feeling like shit—sad and lost and hopeless, something had to change for me, and quick.

99.

"Here I am, the wind's a-blowing, and I'm jamming away, trying to make a few bucks," sang the guy on the Ocean Beach Pier—adjusting his sunglasses, sitting on a bench and strumming a cheap acoustic guitar. The guitar's dark blue finish had LOVE HERE etched into it, probably by a knife.

He had to almost yell because the waves were high and crashing.

"I can barely hear you," I said.

"It's the music of nature, dude," he told me, "the ocean is my back-up band. BOOM, BOOM, BOOM—like drums, you know?"

"Do you make any money out here?" I asked.

"Used to jam next to the Starbucks, which was better. Cops chase me away. Too close to the ATM machine, makes people nervous. Hell, some lady the other day left her bankcard in the machine and I coulda cleaned her out. But nooooo, I turned it in to the bike cops. That's the *right* thing to do. I'm an honest dude just trying to make some coinage."

The right thing to do, I thought.

"I'll play you a song," he said, "a Dylan song. Like to hear a Bob Dylan song?"

He played "Like a Rolling Stone." He had the chords down, but got lost in the lyrics.

I gave him what I had in my pocket: a buck and a quarter.

100.
That night, I did what Melody asked me never to do: I went to see her dance.

She was taking drink orders when I walked in. I stood in back, in the dark, so she wouldn't see me. Her hair was jet black; that wasn't a wig. I wondered when she'd dyed it, again. She was wearing a pink dress that barely covered her ass, a black g-string and white go-go boots. She chatted it up with a few men and I felt something in my heart. Jealousy? Hate?—and for whom: Melody or the men that lusted after her with their dark and beady eyes? She went in back, where I knew she would change. The DJ announced her stage name: "Gentlemen and nasty boys, welcome back on stage our very own sassy cowgirl Valerie!" She jumped up on stage with a cowboy hat, cowboy boots, and little white shirt and extremely tight red short-shorts, two toy pistols holstered on her shapely hip. She did the three dance number routine: the first song she remained clothed, took out her guns now and then; the second songs the guns and the top came off, and she shook her tits and said, "yeeehaw!" a lot; the third song the shorts came off—she wore a g-string. Not a single pubic hair peeked out, and although it was against the law, she did pull the g-string back for a second, showing men a very brief glimpse of her pussy. I saw it—it was a cunt I knew and missed. This is when Melody saw me, because I was sitting right at the front of the stage. I laid a five-dollar bill down. She stopped for a moment and I saw confusion, pain and anger in her eyes. She quickly glossed her eyes over. She leaned down to pick up the bill and said, loud enough for me to hear, "Meet me outside, *now*." I got up and left. Melody joined me a few minutes later, wearing a long leather coat.

"When did you get that," I said.

She swung and punched me in the mouth.

"Shit," I said, tasting blood.

"What did I tell you? What did I tell you?"

"I couldn't help myself."

"I don't want you to see me in that fucking hellhole!"

"I know but Melody—"

"Did you *like* seeing me in there? How I have to *be*?"

"No," I said, "no I didn't."

"You see?!"

"Hear me out."

"No. *I hate you*."

"Please."

"Just *go home*, Georgie. Go home or I'll send a bouncer out, and you *don't* want that."

101.

Once I got home, I wanted to kill myself. I contemplated the many ways I could do it. The phone rang. It was Melody:

"I didn't mean anything I said. I was just *so*…. I don't know. Can you forgive me? Sorry I decked you."

"I guess I had it coming," I said.

"You did, boy. Tell me you love me."

I told her.

I waited.

"You know I feel the same," she said. "We love each other."

"Yes."

"You would do anything for me and I would do anything for you."

"Yes."

"We're soul mates," she said. "Listen, Georgie. There's something you need to do. That I want you to do. That you have to do, for both our sakes."

"Anything," I said. "Name it."

"I get off at one. I'm leaving here with this guy I know."

"Who?"

"No one."

"Who is he?"

"He's just some guy. He's rich, and that's good for us."

"What am I supposed to do?"

"He has a boat at the Marina. Downtown, where you are."

"Okay."

"I'm going there with him. We'll be there by one-thirty. I want you to be there by two."

"How—"

"*Listen*. His boat is called *Debbie G*. Dock J. I'll make sure the gate is ajar. Wear your gloves. Sneak onto the boat. We'll be below deck. I'll make sure he's distracted."

"And then?"

"And *then* you're gonna knock him out and we're gonna *rob* this asshole...."

102. Gaslamp Marina, near Seaport Village shopping mall and the Marriott Hotel.

Dozens of yachts of all sizes. Jerry Lewis' yacht was docked here. The gate to Dock J wasn't locked, like she said. I walked down the thin pier, wood creaking below my feet; found *Debbie G*. three boats down. It was a fifty-footer, no sail. A beautiful boat, and being so near it made me feel small and ugly; made me feel like a failure and like I hadn't done shit with my shitty life. I also felt anger, confusion, jealousy and everything evil that comes up from the gut thinking about Melody being with whoever owned this boat. Who was this lucky devil and what was he doing with my girl? I put the gloves on and hopped onto the boat, trying to be as quiet as possible. There was a light on in the cabin; I could hear soft jazz music. And voices, sounds. I crept below deck. Moaning. That was Melody. And some guy grunting, the two of them laughing. My blood ran fast and hot, I wanted to scream, I wanted to kill. I spotted an unopened bottle of white wine, picked it up. I moved toward the voices. On a small bed, two naked people. Melody and a man with gray hair and a flabby body—he was in his fifties. What was she doing with a man that old? Why was she screwing him? He was on top of her and plunging his cock inside and out of her pussy, his skinny ass moving back and forth, Melody's legs up on his shoulders. She opened her eyes and saw me. We stared at each other for only a second but it seemed like an hour. She nodded her head, her mouth said a silent yes and then she said, "Do it, just do it," and the man said, "I am doing it, baby," and I said, "Hey, asshole."

He sat up, said, "What the hell?" He looked at me and said, "What the hell?"

Melody screamed. I wanted to hit *her* with the bottle I was so pissed. But I hit the man instead, on the side of his head, sticking to the plan. The bottle shattered, glass and wine splattered and scattered all over the bed and on Melody. The man went down, unconscious.

He lay on the bed, his mouth open, his head bleeding.

"Oh my," I said, "did I kill him?"

Melody stood on the bed, looking shocked.

"Did I kill him?"

"No, he's breathing," she said.

And then she clapped her hands.

"Good job, Georgie."

"You were doing him," I said.

"We have to act fast."

"You were—"

"Georgie," she said, coming to me, making sure not to step on any pieces of glass, *"listen,"* and she touched my face, "we don't have time to talk about this. I know where he keeps his money. His wife has no idea about this boat— his little fuck pad—or his mad cash. But I do. And it's a good score."

She walked into the tiny galley. I have to say watching her naked body was nice, and *I* wanted to fuck her right then and there. She opened a bottom cabinet and removed a small bundle of money that was in shrink-wrap.

She handed it to me.

"Holy moola, Batman," I said.

"That's right, boy."

"How much is this?"

This was all hundred-dollar bills.

"Frank says he always keeps twenty grand stashed for an emergency. Stupid fool, he bragged about it, like it would *impress* me. It impressed me all right. Now it's... *ours*."

"Frank?"

"*Who* do you *think*?"

I looked at the man, still unconscious on the bed.

"Take that too," Melody said, nodding at a watch on the counter.

I picked it up. "Nice."

"That's a Rolex, boy, and it's *real*. No knock-off."

"We can't sell this," I said. "He probably has the serial number."

"I want you to *wear* it, not hock it." She smiled and tilted her head. "You should have a fancy watch. Why not? It'll look nice on you."

I pocketed the thing.

"Now go pick up his pants from the floor and clean out his wallet," she told me. "Make this look like a bona fide robbery."

I got out the wallet. His ID said his name was Franklin Davidson. He also had a hospital ID. He was some kind of doctor. There was $240 in twenties plus a few $1 bills. I folded these, put them in my pocket, and tossed the wallet on top of the good doctor's naked, pale back.

Melody kissed me. It was a good, long kiss and I grabbed her ass. (I also kept in mind that she'd been humping the doctor just a few minutes ago.)

"You did good," she said.

"Get dressed," I said, "let's get out of here."

"I have to stay."

"What?"

"Think, boy, *think*," she said. "I have to stay and play this out. A burglar came, he was robbed. I'll say the big nasty burglar molested me. He won't call the cops, he won't risk his wife finding out about his hideaway and the spare cash. But if I leave he'll suspect I set him up. Then he *might* call the cops. Or he'll come to the club and cause trouble for me—the owners don't take kindly to girls who roll the customers. I can't just quit the club because that would look suspicious too. You understand?"

I nodded.

"Now, there's something you have to do. You *really* have to do this, okay?"

"What," I said.

"Hit me. Give me a good one on my face. Give me a black eye. I have to look like a victim, too. Frank will feel for me. The money, the watch, he won't give a shit if he thinks he got me hurt."

"Hit you," I said.

"Yes," she said.

It was easy. I was so mad that I let it all out in that punch. I didn't give her a shiner, but a bloody lip and a loose tooth. She fell back on the floor with a hard thump.

She looked up at me, surprised.

"Melody," I said, feeling like a lump of coal.

"Now scram," she said.

103.

She knocked on my door just after dawn. I couldn't sleep. Her make-up was smeared and she had a dark bruise near her mouth and dried blood on her lower lip. She hugged me. I tried to kiss her but she said: "Don't—it hurts. You socked me good."

"I'm sorry."

"It was necessary." She looked at the spoils of our crime that I'd neatly placed on the bed. *"Money,"* she said.

"There's a lot."

She squealed, jumped up and down, took my hands in hers and said, "C'mon, Georgie boy, it's celebration day!"

"Wait," I said, "wait," I held her still. "What happened? What did he say? What did *you* say?"

"It played well. He figured a scumbag was hanging around the docks to burn someone. It happens now and then, he said. And he didn't want to call the cops, he was more concerned that I was hurt. In fact," she said with a giggle, "he says he's going to give me five grand, just to make sure I'm hush about all this. If his wife ever found out, he's fucked."

"And you were fucking him."

"Listen, I had to. It had to look real."

"You'd been to that boat before," I said.

"Yeah."

"How many times?"

"Does it matter?"

"How long have you been fucking that doctor?"

"Let's not go there," she said.

"How *long*?"

"It's *over*, okay? *I won't go to that boat anymore.*"

"Are there others?"

"Georgie, why are you—"

I wanted to hit her...again.

She could see this.

"Do it," she said, "hurt me like my uncle did."

"I can't stand it," I told her. "That's all."

"It doesn't matter, those assholes don't matter. They're just a source of income. And look at all we have," she pointed at the money. "*Twenty grand*. With another *five* coming. And this," she picked up the Rolex and clasped it to my wrist. "You deserve this, okay? You do. Not him. *You.*"

I held up my arm and looked at the watch.

"You like?" she asked.

I said, "Yes."

She opened the shrink-wrapped money. She spread the bills out on the bed.

104.

We rolled around in all those $100 bills. I said, "How do we split it? 50/50?"

"First, we're going to get you out of this shit-hole room," she said, "and we're going to get an apartment."

"We?"

"You and me. A real place. The hell with that. Let's rent a house, a real home. A place to call home, for once. Does that sound good, Georgie?"

"You and me?"

"What, you don't want to live with me?"

105.
"There are more," she said later, "more dumb assholes we can rob."

"More of these...men," I said.

"Yes," I said.

"How many?"

"There is an endless supply. They come and go."

"Who are they?"

"Fools," she said, "who come in to see some booty, who try to seduce the dancers—me—and who deserve to be mugged. Are you up for it, Georgie? We can make enough money so I won't have to work, and you won't, and we can kick it in comfort and be really happy."

"I just don't want you to fuck them," I said.

"I won't," she said. "The only thing that'll get fucked is their heads and their pocketbooks."

"We'll be criminals," I said.

"We are. We always were."

I couldn't argue with that truth.

She said, "I hate the way they look at me. I just can't stand it. They look at me the way Uncle Pete did and they think they can own me by waving money in my face. I want to *show* them, Georgie. I want some more *revenge.*"

106.
First, we rented a cozy two-bedroom house in Hillcrest. We paid six months

rent in cash and the landlord smiled and said there was no need to do a credit check, we seemed like a nice enough young couple. "This is home," Melody said, her voice echoing throughout the empty house, "wow."

I said, "Wow?"

She looked at me and said, "Yeah, wow."

I smiled and she smiled.

We embraced and kissed and the next thing we both knew, we were having a quickie on the cold, hardwood floor....

107.

Melody felt we should celebrate our new life together. "We deserve it," she said, "so we should treat ourselves to some goodies." She went shopping for new clothes: shoes and skirts and blouses and bras. I was happy to be with her, watch her try on things, model for me. Hey, I was a man in love, what can I say? I was happy to no longer be alone.

So we went from one mall to another—Horton Plaza to Fashion Valley to University Town Center, these complexes of commerce where we spent, spent, spent.

The backseat and truck of my car were stuffed.

"But what about you, Georgie?" she said, caressing the side of my face with one hand and squeezing my crotch with the other. "You haven't gotten anything."

"I don't need to."

"Bull."

"I don't."

"Isn't there *some*thing you want, boy?"

"Just you, girl," I said; I enjoyed watching her slowly blush.

"Really," she said, "we have that asshole's cash. Let's *spend it....*"

"Maybe I could get my Mustang tuned up, new brake pads, rotate the tires...."

"Isn't there *some* material thing your silly heart secretly desires?" she asked, nuzzling her nose into my neck. "That you could never afford before...?"

108.
I told her that I always wanted a guitar. I didn't know how to play—just knew a few basic chords from having fiddled with the guitars of people I knew. I had no desire to be in a band, I just liked the way the instrument felt in my hands, how it sounded, how it looked.

"So let's go get you a fucking axe," she said, and we drove to a music store in Clairmont Mesa with a bundle of cash.

It was a big store, and the sound of people trying out guitars, basses and drums filled my head and made my brain and eyes pound.

I noticed plenty of men look at Melody and I didn't blame them—her mini-skirt, let long legs, her dark hair, the way she walked. I liked how she held my hand and told one of the sales guys: "We want to buy something."

"For you," the salesman said, "or—"

"Him," she said.

The salesman looked disappointed. "Okay."

He showed us many instruments, and I loved them all. I didn't know anything—what was good, what was the right price.

"He needs to learn how to play," Melody said, "but he needs something top-notch."

He looked at our tattoos and asked, "Are you rockabilly types?"

We both shrugged.

"I have the guitar in mind," he said, "a hollow-body Gretch. It's a beauty."

The guitar in question was. It was big and pale blue with gold hardware.

"What do you think?" Melody asked me.

"I love it," I said.

"We'll take it," she told the salesman.

"Don't you want to know how much?" he asked.

"How much?"

"Well, it retails for $1,200, but I can let you have it for $900."

"Okay," and she shrugged, getting the money out of her purse.

"I need an amp too," I whispered to her.

"We need one of those amp things," Melody said. "What do you recommend?"

"Um," the salesman said, calculating his commission inside his head, "this Fender amp right here would be good, $600."

"Sounds cool."

"And maybe some effects pedals? Flange, phase-shifting, and a fuzz pedal?"

"Baby?" Melody looked up at me and batted her eyelashes.

I said, "Yeah."

The total was two grand plus tax. We gave the salesman a $100 tip, which he quickly pocketed, making sure his fellow employees didn't see.

"Rock 'n' roll!" he said as we left.

109.

"I have another rich idiot lined up," she said.

"Okay," I said.

"What's wrong?" she asked.

"Nothing," I said.

"Look, we can make some more money here," she said.

"Money," I said, "sure."

110.

Even though I played like shit, I liked plugging my guitar into the amplifier and strumming at the strings. It had a beautiful sound, especially in our new home. I think the hardwood floors assisted in the acoustics.

111.

Melody asked, "What is it, boy? What's on your mind?"

"I want you to stop dancing at that place."

"I know."

"So *stop*."
"Soon," she said. *"Soon."*
I groaned and turned away from her.

112. "We need to score," she said.
"Yeah," I said.

113. Frank the boatman came into the club and asked Melody how she was doing, and she told him she was all right. How was he? She was worried. Or so she said. "I play my part well." He said he was sorry for what happened and slipped her $500 in $50 bills.

"He hasn't come into the club since," Melody told me.
I nodded and whispered, "Good."

114. *"So,"* said my parole officer.
"Things are wonderful," I said. "I have a home, and I'm in love."

She looked surprised. "Really."
"Really."
"Man or woman?"
I sighed.
She said, "I have to ask."
"Woman."
"Where did you meet her?"

"We've always known each other," I said.

"Really?"

"Since we were kids."

"What does she do?"

"Sales," I said.

"Is this good?" I was asked.

I said, "It is."

115.

So this is what happened: she said there was this man who was sweet on her. He was recently divorced, forty, had sold a company he co-owned and was rich. "He keeps wanting to fly me away to Vegas, Atlantic City, Paris. He says he can see me as wife #2."

Something hurt in my chest. "He just wants to fuck you."

"Yeah," she said, like: and so?

"Have you?"

"Oh, Georgie."

She rolled her eyes.

We looked at each other.

"So," she said.

"So tell me what you want me to do," I said.

"He's coming in tonight. I'll act like I've caved in to his charm. I'll go home with him. Don't worry, I won't have sex. That is, if you get there in time. What I'll do is get up and act like I left something in his car, I'll say: 'Just give me the keys and I'll get it.' Then I'll leave the door to his place unlocked. Then you'll come in and do your thing."

"But you've never been to his house, right?"

"Right. No."

"So how do you know where he keeps his money?"

"He's *told* me," she said, leaning in close so I could smell the perfume and soap on her skin, "he always tells me how he's bought a shit load of bars of gold and how I should see them with my very own eyes. And that's what I plan to do. He shows me the gold, and then the gold will be ours."

That night, at eleven, Melody called on her cell phone. "It's a go," she said, and gave me the address to this guy's house in a suburban neighborhood called Tierrasanta. "I should be there by midnight," she said, "so you be ready an hour later."

"Why an hour?"

"I need an hour, this has to look smooth, not like a set-up."

"Okay."

"And Georgie...don't hurt him too bad. Just knock him out."

I was there well before midnight. I waited in my car. A black SUV pulled up and Melody got out with the man—he was tall and slim and partially bald and dressed real nice: a stylish leather jacket and well-creased slacks. She took his arm as they went inside. My heart was going fast, I felt vehement; I tried to maintain control....

Forty-five minutes later, Melody slipped out of the house, jingling keys and giggling. I could tell by the way she was walking that she was buzzed.

I moved up behind her.

She jumped. "Jesus Christ on roller-skates," she said, her voice low, "don't *do* that!"

I could smell bourbon on her breath.

"You're drunk," I said.

"So what," she said, "you ready?"

"I'm ready."

"Fifteen, twenty minutes, okay?"

"Kiss me."

She did.

I tasted her lipstick and the booze.

"Gold," she reminded me.

"Did you see it?"

"There's a *lot*, and it's pretty."

She went back into the house and I returned to my car. I waited exactly fifteen minutes. I put on my gloves, went to the trunk, and got out a piece of thick rope.

I casually walked up to the door. It was unlocked.

Music. They always play music, these seducers.

It was a nice house, though.

Very big.

I hated him, whoever he was, for the things he had; for making me want to steal what he had.

The man and Melody were in the living room, on the couch, making out.

Kissing with too much passion.

Melody opened her eyes and saw me.

I was behind the man.

She pulled away from him and said, "Oh my God, Henry—"

Before he could do anything, I had the rope around his neck and was choking him.

He put up a good struggle. We rolled around on the floor. I tightened the grip.

"Stop!" Melody said. "You're killing him!"

Henry's body went limp. I let go.

"Oh, Georgie," Melody said, "did you kill him?"

"No. He's just out."

"Are you sure?"

"Very," I said. "It's a trick I learned in prison."

116.
The rule for choking a man into unconsciousness was: *let go when you smell shit.* That's what Ron told me. Some big fucker jumped me once, tried to rape me, and Ron came to my rescue, choking the guy with his rolled-up shirt.

Henry was smelly all right—he'd crapped his pants.

"Ugh," Melody said, pinching her nose.

"Where's the gold?" I asked.

"Over here," she said, walking behind the bar.

There were so many bottles...all expensive stuff.

"Look at this booze," I said.

"Take some."

I planned to.

She said, "Come look at this, boy. The bars are under the bar."

I joined her. There were forty-five bricks of solid gold. I whistled.

She handed me one. "Feel it."

It was heavy, smooth, cold, clean.

"How much do these go for?"

"I don't know."

"You think we can get some good money for them?"

"Yeah," she said, "I do."

117.

We left with the gold and a few bottles of Chivas Regal.

"That went easy," she said. "Too easy, maybe."

"Do you think he'll suspect?" I said.

"I don't know. I have to quit that club."

"Quit dancing?" I said hopefully.

"I'll go to another club," she said, "there are more targets out there. A few more, and we'll live *good*, Georgie."

"So how are we going to sell this gold? We can't just waltz into a bank. Or a pawn shop...."

"I know someone—I think he might like to buy them."

"Who?"

118.

She made some phone calls. A week later, a man from Los Angeles came down to take a look at the gold. I didn't know who he was, how and why Melody knew him; he didn't give a name and she didn't say his name. They nodded at each other and both said, "Been a while." He was thirty, round boyish face and stone cold killer eyes. He wore a black suit and a thin tie. He carried a satchel. We showed him the bars of gold. He inspected several closely, said, "Very nice," with a strange accent, Eastern European maybe—what did I know. I'd never been anywhere outside San Diego except the pen. I was wondering what we'd say if he asked where we got the gold bars. He didn't. What he said was: "I can give you ten thousand."

"How about eleven?" Melody said.

"Certainly. But no more."

She looked at me. "Well?"

I shrugged.

"Deal," she said.

The man reached into his satchel. I almost expected a gun. He came out with eleven stacks of twenties, each stack a grand....

119.

Melody jumped up and down when the guy left. She tossed one of the stacks up—bills landed all around us like fallen angels.

"Was that easy money or what?" she said. "Or *what*?"

"Look," I said, "who the hell was that dude?"

"Does it matter?"

I shrugged.

"*Hey,* I never *fucked* him, *okay*?" She was angry.

"Did we get a good price? How do we know—?"

"It was a low price, but the shit is hot and he has to sell it and make his own profit. Eleven g's isn't bad for one night's work, Georgie boy."

"I just wonder how you know a guy like that."

"You'd be surprised at some of the criminals I know from Los Angeles," she said, "and they're all involved, one way or another, in porn."

"Oh," I said.

"I'm glad I'm away from *that* scene...."

120. She went to work at a different strip club, on Ohio Street, part-time: two nights a week. It didn't take long before she found a victim, a widower who fell in love with her (so he said) during the first lap dance she gave him. So we rolled the guy. And the next. After about a month of this, we had plenty of cash horded away and I told her she should stop dancing, we could kick back and relax. "That sounds good," she said, "I could use the rest."

And then I got a letter that changed everything.

121. The letter was waiting for me at my downtown mailbox. I'd rented the box when I was moving about motel rooms after my release. I only picked up my mail twice a month because there was hardly ever anything pressing to deal with, if I had mail at all. The letter was from Ron Hoagland. His was getting out and wanted to come down to San Diego and look me up, which had always been the plan. The letter was sent a week ago and he was scheduled to be set free in three days! I had always planned to be there for him the minute he stepped away from the gates, and I would.

122. "I really want to meet this guy," Melody said.

"Oh, you will," I said.

123.

I embraced Ron, outside Concoran State Prison. He said, "It's damn good to see ya, kiddo. This your ride?"

"She's mine."

We got into my car and he said, "It's damn good to be free."

"Freedom is...nice," and I smiled and laughed and we both laughed and he turned around and gave the prison the finger and yelled:

"I HOPE YOU ALL DIE!"

I felt the same.

"You drove all the way here," he said.

"Of course."

"It looks like freedom has been good for you, kiddo."

"It has."

"Tell me."

So I told him.

He raised his brows and whistled. "So you got a lady."

"I mentioned her before. My old girlfriend...."

"Yeah, you two were kids...."

"I guess."

"Now?"

"We're together. And we're not kids anymore."

"Is it serious?" he asked.

"Serious enough," I said.

124.

Melody said, "Georgie has told me so much about you, Ron, that I almost feel like I know you," and she embraced him, hard. Ron looked at me—I saw pain in his eyes. Having a woman this close right after getting out can drive a man to do crazy things. Like come in his pants. I could see Ron was trying to maintain his cool.

"You smell very nice," Ron said, softly.

She stepped back. "It's a new brand I got this morning. You like it, Georgie?"

"Yes," I said. "I told Ron he could crash on the couch until he figures out what to do. Is this cool?"

"Hey, he saved your life, didn't he? You owe him, which means so do I." She winked at Ron. "Our casa is su casa and all that."

"Thanks," Ron said, looking uncomfortable.

She said, "Georgie didn't tell me you're such a handsome devil."

"Well," said Ron, "he did tell me how beautiful you are."

"He *better* have," and she hit me in the arm.

125.

Later that night, Melody gave me a blowjob and then said, "It must be very difficult for him."

"What?"

"You know what. One thing I know is how to read men. Read them like menus. How to see pain and...desire. Or need. How long has it been since he's had a girl?"

We looked at each other for a long minute and there was an understanding between us.

"Go do it," I said.

"Are you sure?"

"Yes."

"It feels like the right thing to do."

"Go and fuck him good," I said.

She stood up. "I plan to fuck his brains out." She was wearing a T-shirt and panties. She removed both, stood before me naked. "How do I look?"

"Wonderful."

"This will be a nice gift for him, yeah?"

"Yeah," I said.

She left the bedroom. I heard some mumbling and it didn't take long for them to go at it. The sounds of sex lasted about five minutes, then stopped. I expected her to return but she didn't. Then I heard Ron groaning and saying, "Suck it, baby, get it hard again," and then they were both making hot-'n'-wet noises, and they were very loud. Melody's resonance was different, not the way she sounded with me. She was—I don't know what: primal....

I couldn't take any more. I was going to lose it, do something stupid. I got dressed and walked out. They were on the floor. Melody legs were wrapped around his neck and Ron was slamming his pelvis into her, hard, flesh slapping together, her fingernails clawing at his back. Ron was saying: "Pump that pussy, baby, pump it...."

They saw me and stopped.

"Joining in, kiddo?" Ron asked. "We gonna tag team your sweetheart?"

"I'm going out," I said, heading for the door.

"Join us," Melody said. "Please."

"You cool with this, kiddo?" Ron said.

"It's cool," I said, walking out, and it was: Ron needed this and I knew I'd eventually get over it....

126.

I walked around the block half a dozen times, then I went up to University Avenue to a bar called Alibi. I sat down and had two schooner-sized beers. Then I had a shot of te-quila. I walked around some more. Three hours. That should've been enough time.

Home, Ron was snoring on the couch, naked. The place stank of fuck. Melody was in the bedroom. She wasn't asleep. There were bruises on her face and neck.

"No," I said.

"It's okay. Sometimes I like it rough."

"This is weird," I said.

"Come here," she said, pulling me to her.

"Melody," I said.

"I want some *more*," she said, "I want you now. *You should've stayed.* It would've been fun...."

127.

Melody slept in. I didn't sleep at all. When I heard Ron take a shower and putter about the house, I got up.

"How is she?" he asked.

"Resting."

"I got carried away...."

"She's fine."

"I want to thank you," he said.

"You would've done the same for me."

"Would I? Give you my woman?" He smiled. "You know, you're right."

"What are you doing?"

"I need to go. Get on with my life. Gotta check in with my parole officer. There are some people who owe me. Get a place."

"You can stay here," I said.

"I don't think that will work," he said, "you know."

I nodded. I knew.

We embraced.

"I'll let you know where I am once I'm set up," he said.

When Melody woke up two hours later, she asked about Ron. I told her.

"That's too bad," she said.

"You want him again," I said.

"I want to have you both at the same time," she said, "I think it'd be fantastic. But I also think it'd be a very bad idea."

I didn't say anything.

"We'll have to call it a one-night stand," she said, "and forget about it...."

128. I tried to, but I couldn't. I couldn't get the way she sounded out of my head—

129.

A week later, Ron had an apartment in Pacific Beach, two blocks away from the ocean, which wasn't bad. He called and gave me his number and address.

"P.B. isn't cheap," I said.

"Like I said, there were some people who owed me. And I like it by the water, I can go down to the boardwalk and see all the teenage chicks in their thong bikinis. Man, *the bodies*."

"I bet."

"You and the lady should come by for dinner. I mean, she's the one who suggested I move to this part of town."

"She used to live here, too."

"Both of you, come on over and we'll eat and laugh."

When I told Melody about the invite, she said, "Maybe that's not the best idea."

"Yeah," I said.

She kissed me on the forehead. "Go see your friend. I don't need to be there."

130.

I smoked some hash with Ron. His apartment was big and empty. He had two beanbags and a radio in the living room, and a lone mattress in the bedroom.

"It's nice to smoke good shit," he said, "and not crappity, crap, crap that we got inside."

I was pretty high and all I could do was laugh and nod.

"Things going good?" he said. "You and Melody."

"Sure...."

He nodded.

"She had a bunch of errands, you know," I said.

"I know," he said. "She's a good woman, kiddo...you know."

"She is," I said.

"Not like this *cunt* I have for a parole officer."

I guess I should've asked him about the cunt but I was only interested in smoking more hash....

131.

It's funny how fast money can go, when you think you have enough to stay comfortable for a while and suddenly it starts to dwindle because you're spending it like it's always going to be there. Junk started to pile up in our little house, and when Melody I both agreed we had to curb our spending sprees, we'd go out and buy more clothes and knick-knacks and guitars and high platform shoes. She had seventy pairs of shoes in the closet and I told her: "*This* is ridiculous."

"It's time for us to go back to work," she said.

132.

I got a job running a swing-shift cash register at an Arco gas station—mostly to show my parole officer that I was gainfully employed—and Melody went back to an all nude strip club in Lemon Grove called Tens—a little place near El Cajon and just as dirty and smelly as any East County shit hole—to find our next wealthy, lovelorn, middle-aged victim.

After a week, she said, "No one yet."

A week later: "No one."

The following week: "I should change clubs," and she went to another strip joint, Little Darlin's.

133.
I thought I'd surprise Ron by showing up at his door with a bottle of Johnny Walker Red, his favorite scotch. I also needed to talk to him; I needed a father confessor about what was going on with Melody, see what his take was. I was prepared to tell him the truth about my crimes.

I *wasn't* prepared for what I saw, what I discovered—Ron answered, sweaty and smelling like booze, hash and fuck. "Hey, kiddo, why didn't you call," and a woman's voice said: "Babe, who is it?"

I knew that voice.

A woman came out from the bedroom, holding a wrapped sheet around her naked body.

I *knew* that woman....

It was Sandra O'Connell, my—our—parole officer.

"Oh shit," she said, and rushed back to the bedroom.

"Bad timing?" I said.

"Something like that," Ron said.

"She says good things about you," he said.

"She says nothing about you," I said. "I didn't even know we were sharing the same...P.O."

Ron smiled. "The woman is discreet, what can I say...."

134.

"I can't help it," Ron told me on the phone later, "I like the ladies and they like me." He sighed melodramatically. "Got a lot of catching up to do."

"But she's..." I laughed. It was, all in all, very funny.

"Yeah, so?"

"Isn't that *dangerous*?" I asked.

"It helps," he said. "Now I can get away with murder."

135.

"So," Sandra O'Connell said, crossing her legs, looking very uncomfortable. Her face slowly became red as we sat there in her stuffy little office....

"My life is good," I said, "and the job is swell. How about you?" I asked, adding: "Mrs. O'Connell."

"Look," she said.

"Yes?" I said.

"What you saw," she said.

"Yes," I said.

"You *didn't* see it," she said, stern and serious. "Understand me?"

Pause.

"Yeah," I said, "I do."

"I hope so," she said.

I knew this would be the last time I'd ever see her....

136.

"Something's come up, it's crazy but this could be our last and big score," Melody said. "Hear me out, okay?"

I said okay.

She said, "There's this guy I did some X-rated movies for—"

"Another one," I said with dismay.

"I wouldn't exactly call it *porn*, I mean *he* called it *art*. It was strange stuff. What did he say it was? Oh yes—'surreal.' 'Porn on the edge' or whatever. Anyway, it was a gig and he paid and it was unusual stuff, it was kinda like acting; there was a script and some dialogue and I guess there was a story, what *he* thought was a story...."

"Why are you telling me this?"

"He doesn't make any money doing these movies and has no backers. So the way he finances them...he prints funny money."

"What?"

"Counterfeit bills."

"No shit."

"No shit. And I...kinda used to help him."

"Help him how? Mix the ink?"

"I was a mule."

"And he was a cowboy?"

"I helped him move money, make deals."

"So this guy's an ex-boyfriend?"

"Not exactly. But we were friends."

"Good friends?"

"Good enough. Why are you acting like this?"

"Why are you telling me about him?"

"He called the other day," Melody sighed. "He said... he missed me. Missed doing movies...and helping his transactions. See, if there's a pretty girl holding the money, exchanging the counterfeit bag for the buy bag, the other side feels better, more at ease, you know. They can look at my legs and ass, I smile, they don't think I have a gun...."

"Okay."

"He called and asked me to mule again, just this one time. It's a big score, he says. It'll finance his next five projects. He's printed up a million bucks of phony twenties and hundreds for $100,000 of the real thing."

I whistled.

"You got it," she said.

"What are you thinking?"

"We fry him. $100,000 will last us quite a while, boy."

I agreed.

"We can even leave San Diego and start life all over somewhere," she said. "Move to the desert, like Arizona or New Mexico. Ever been to New Mexico? It's very beautiful out there...."

"You've been?"

"I've seen pictures."

137.

She showed me three of the tapes this dude made. *A Ted Smythe Film* they all claimed. Written, Produced and Directed by. The titles: *The Twilight of Illusion*, *West of Babylon*, *Beyond the Beyond*. Hard-to-follow story lines, strange electronic music, lots of extreme close-ups. There was a science-fiction/ alien/vampire theme to them, Melody was the star. And there was sex—lots of cock-sucking and a twisted fetish for sodomy. I didn't like them at all. I wasn't sure what Melody felt.

"They're...different," she said.

"Guy who makes movies like this," I said, "deserves to be jacked."

138. Two days later, Melody told me the deal:

"Teddy—"

"Teddy?"

"He's just a bear."

"Give me a break."

"Ted," she said, "has this shady lawyer who hooks him up with buyers—it's not like Ted knows real criminals, he only knows how to print the funny money. This lawyer, Max Waxman," she shook her head, "a real goober, I hope I never have to deal with him again—anyway, a meet has been set up in six days. Teddy—Ted—will have the bills ready by then. I'll need to go up to L.A. ahead of time, smooth things out, confer how the exchange is gonna go down...."

"I see."

I was not pleased.

"Oh *shit*, Georgie," she said, irritated, "I'm not gonna *fuck* the guy. I've *never* fucked the Teddy Bear. He just likes to *watch.*"

139. I tried to get a hold of Ron over the next few days but he wasn't around. Man, I really needed someone to talk to....

140. Melody called. "It's on. Just like we planned."

141. The next day I drove up to Los Angeles, five miles under the speed limit, making sure no Highway Patrol officer took notice of me. At 3:30, I checked into a cheap motel in Culver City. I hated the way this part of L.A. smelled, reminded me of National City or Chula Vista. Or even El Cajon.

At five, Melody showed up. She was dressed like a street whore—spandex pants, high heels, halter top: the works.

"What's this?" I said, giving her the once-over.

"Playing the part," she said.

I *liked* the look—

We kissed—too much lipstick and bubble gum in her mouth—

Oh yes, I liked her this way—

We moved onto the bed and had a quickie—

Then we went over the plan again.

She took out a handgun from her purse.

"It's not loaded," I said.

"It's not even *real*, Georgie boy. But it sure looks real, huh?" she said.

"Real enough."

142.

At eleven that night, I was parked in the lot at Marina del Rey, near all the docked sailboats and yachts. I waited. Waited. At eleven-fifteen, a big old Chevy pulled in. I saw that Melody was in the passenger seat, her dark hair bunched up in a messy bun. The guy sitting next to her—obviously Ted the film auteur—seemed tall, wore thick glasses. When he got out, he was tall. Six-foot-five at least. He went to meet a man who pulled up in a blue Caprice—this fellow was stocky, long red hair pulled back in a ponytail. He was carrying a briefcase. The two had some words. Ted waved. Melody got out the car, carrying a big heavy gym bag that I figured was filled with the phony greenbacks.

"Hey guy," I could hear her voice, "how's it going?"

"Let's see the funny," said the guy with the red ponytail.

"Let's see the bona fide," said Ted.

"You first."

Ted nodded.

Melody set the gym bag down and opened it.

Ponytail man set his briefcase down and opened it.

Melody yawned and said, "Can we get this done so I can get my beauty sleep?"

That was my cue.

I quietly crept out of my car. In one hand, I had the fake gun; in the other, a crowbar.

I crouched down as I made my move.

I was very quick.

I moved behind ponytail as he was still bent down and slammed him across the back on the head with the crowbar. There was a horrible sound of something squishy, and there was blood, and the guy fell.

I pointed the fake gun at Ted. "Don't make a move."

"Do as he says," Melody said.

Ted caught on quick. "You set me up?"

"Sorry, babe."

"I'll kill you for this."

"Look out!" Melody cried.

Ponytail was still conscious. He pulled a badge out from under his shirt. "U.S. Secret Service," he mumbled, moaned, groaned, "you're all under arrest." In his other hand was a revolver. I moved out of the way and he fired. Teddy got it in the face. His face exploded all over the parking lot, and it was not a pretty sight, nor did it smell all that good.

I knocked the revolver out of Ponytail's hand with the crowbar. And then I hit him across the face, smashing his jaw and teeth in.

Melody grabbed the revolver.

She said, "The money!"

I closed the briefcase and took possession.

"What about that?" I asked, pointing at the gym bag.

"Fuck that shit, it's worthless to us," and started toward my car.

I followed.

Two burly guys in suits appeared out of the dark.

"FREEZE! U.S. TREASURY AGENTS! HALT OR WE'LL SHOOT!"

"Damn," Melody said, jumping in the car.

They began to shoot.

I got behind the wheel.

Glass shattered.

Melody fired back three times, hitting one of them.

"DRIVE!" she screamed.

I drove—

143.
"You okay?" she said. "You hit?"

"I'm okay. You?"

"I'm still in one piece."

Then we both laughed....

144.
She was looking out the shattered back window. "Holy crap," she said, "how crazy was that? We set-up a set-up. It was a government sting!"

"Are we being followed?"

"At least the buy money is real," she said.

I said, "Are we being followed?!"

"It doesn't look like it."

"What about choppers? Is there a chopper in the sky? Tailing us?"

She stuck her head out the window. "No."

"You sure?"

"I think you're too paranoid," Melody said, "watch too much TV."

"Bullshit. We—"

"We better get on the freeway fast," she said.

145.

I wasn't paying attention. I drove through a red, my front getting slammed by one of those ridiculously big pick-up trucks with large wheels. The kind baseball-hat wearing jackasses with small dicks like to drive to make them feel big. The Mustang spun around several times. Melody and I both screamed.

When we stopped, Melody and I looked at each other.

"You okay?" we said to each other.

"Look at your car," she said.

The front end was totaled and the engine was steaming.

The big truck was only dented.

The guy who was driving the truck was pissed. He was skinny and wore a baseball cap, in his thirties, and his eyes were red. He had a baseball bat in his hand and was coming our way.

The street was empty; no witnesses.

"You stupid bastard," the guy was saying, "are you blind? Look what you did! I'm gonna mess you up."

He raised the bat and charged.

Melody got out, took a stance, held up the pistol, said, "Fuck you, motherfucker," and shot the man once in the chest.

He went down, the baseball bat bouncing on the pavement—the wood sound echoed, along with the gunshot.

"Oh boy," I said.

"Get the money. We'll take his truck."

I started to say something but she reminded me that my car was now useless. She had a point.

"Can you drive one of these things?" she asked when we got into the big truck with big wheels.

"Oh yeah," I said, and we took off.

146.

The adrenaline didn't wear off. If anything it got worse as we both contemplated what had happened in the span of ten minutes and how many people were dead. We stopped off at a liquor store and got a bottle of tequila, which didn't help to settle our nerves. So we stopped off in a dark area and fucked. That helped. We drank more. We stopped off at a Denny's and had some pancakes and coffee. That helped a little. We drove and stopped again and fucked again and we both felt we had our game back. It was six-thirty in the morning by the time we returned to San Diego. We ditched the truck in La Jolla and called a taxicab. There wasn't an army of cops waiting for us. I told her I didn't think the L.A. cops would put it together so quickly. We both agreed we needed to get the hell out of Dodge, go downtown and take a Greyhound to Imperial County, where we could get another bus to Arizona and start a new life....

147. Melody took a shower and I got some clothes and things ready. I would have to leave my guitars behind—and this was all right, I'd never learn to play them anyway. I could buy more with one hundred grand. I stared at the Treasury agent's revolver, sitting on the table, and was afraid to touch it. I'd get life, the needle, the gas chamber, whatever. So would Melody. But this was not a time to be thinking like this—

148. The shower felt wonderful. I washed away the night's crimes and fear like a Jihadist taking a ritual bath before blowing himself (and others) up. I imagined all the various lives Melody and I would have in Arizona or New Mexico. On the run. Having children. Growing old, keeping our secrets—

149. When I got out of the shower, we had a visitor. It was Ron. He was in the living room with Melody. They were kissing. He saw me. She moved away. Ron had the revolver. He pointed it at me.

"Great score, kiddo," he said. "I could've never done it myself. I'm an old man, you know...."

"You're no *old man*," Melody said, rolling her eyes and punching his arm, "you're just my *Big Daddy*...."

150.

"$100,000 is gonna buy us a new life, kiddo, and I guess I have to thank you," said my old prison chum. He shook his head. "I feel like *shit* doing this to you, but I have no choice...hey, remember what I used to say about The Big Score? It's like the lottery...."

"Only one lucky sucker in a zillion's actually going to get it," I said.

"Never knew I'd be that sucker," he said, pulling Melody toward him, "and that I'd get the chance to suck on this sweet candy."

"The day you brought him over, when I was with him that night," Melody said, "I knew I'd met my soul mate."

The sounds she was making....

"I fell in love," she said, "just like that."

"How long?" I asked.

"Ever since that night, kiddo," Ron said, no shame in his voice.

"I never went back to dancing," Melody said, like an excuse, "when you were at work, I was with my—Ron—my—*Big Daddy* here...."

She could not look at me.

I nodded.

"I see," I said.

Silence.

Silence.

"We came up with a good plan," Ron said.

"It went a little haywire," Melody said, "but, oh...it worked marvelously."

Silence....

"Yeah?" she said.

"Yeah," I said.

She still could not look at me.

"I'm sorry about this, kiddo," Ron said, "but we have to get going. You understand...."

"He...*understands*," Melody said softly. "C'mon..."

Ron raised an eyebrow and asked me: "Do you?"

"Yeah," I said with a shrug, looking at the dusty wood floor.

Ron cocked the gun. He was crying. I counted in my head—Ponytail fired once, Melody fired three times at the Treasury agents and once at the man in the big truck....

One bullet left.

ABOUT THE AUTHOR

MICHAEL HEMMINGSON writes books in every possible genre he can: literary, western, SF, horror, noir, autobiography, erotica, narrative journalism, gonzo journalism, cultural anthropology, critical theory, critifiction, ethnography, and many other modes of academia including post-postmodern and postcolonial treatises. And private eye yarns. And film and TV studies. And smut. He also writes plays and screenplays. He has two independent feature films out: *The Watermelon* (LightSong Films) and *Stations* (Hemlene Entertainment). He has produced, directed, and written plays in San Diego and Los Angeles for the Fritz Theater and The Alien Stage Project. He lives in southern California, going back and forth from Hollywood to Ocean Beach, to Encinitas to Pasadena.

www.ingramcontent.com/pod-product-compliance
Lightning Source LLC
Chambersburg PA
CBHW020654180626
46816CB00003B/1283